THE KALEIDOSCOPE GIRL

SHELBIE MAE

Copyright Page

The Kaleidoscope Girl by Shelbie Mae

shelbie-mae.com

© 2019 Shelbie Mae

Cover by Jamielynnecreative.com

Print Book ISBN: 978-1-7334715-0-3

Ebook ISBN: 978-1-7334715-1-0

❀ Created with Vellum

Dedicated to every girl who has struggled to find her beauty in this broken world and who has fought the darkness in her own mind.

TRIGGER WARNING

The Kaleidoscope Girl contains content regarding eating disorders that some in recovery may find triggering. If you are struggling with an eating disorder please contact the National Eating Disorder Association helpline at (800) 931-2237 or find a mental health professional in your area who can help you take steps toward healing.

Chapter 1

P*resent*
   January 2nd, 2018

NOT EVERY SEVENTEEN-YEAR-OLD girl requires weekly meetings with a personal counselor. But I am not most girls, and the confession I'm about to make—which has me fidgeting in my seat—will solidify the fact that I need Kelly.

She relaxes in her grey suede chair, a cup of coffee on the table beside her. Steam rises from the sky blue mug and dissipates. Kelly waits, because she knows me well enough to know I'm about to speak.

My jaw wobbles as I open my mouth. I sit as still as a I can, because I don't want my squirming to prove to Kelly how nervous I am. "I've been fighting with Anna again," I finally confess.

Kelly's expression doesn't change. "Have your behaviors changed?"

I reach for the cup of fruity green tea on the side table and take a sip. "A little. I thought I killed her." I keep the cup between my shaking palms. "I don't know what to do." I hesitate before adding, "I'm scared."

"Scared of what?"

The pomegranate scent that comes from my mug entices me to take a sip. Smooth, green tea, with hints of exotic fruit, slides down my tight throat. Hearing Anna's voice weakens me, and I'm not sure I can kill that piece of myself again.

I share my fears with Kelly. "I'm afraid she'll kill me this time instead of the other way around."

Anna is the name I have assigned to my eating disorder, the one I was diagnosed with five years ago. It's short for anorexia, but I added an *N* for a sliver of humanity. I prefer the name *Anna* instead of *Ana*. I killed her five months ago. Four of those months were spent in treatment. But now I'm out, and now she's back, and there are no guarantees she won't end me this time. She would kill me slowly. My death could take years. Eating disorders have the highest mortality rate out of all mental illnesses. And I have one.

Anna.

My enemy. My friend.

Myself.

Kelly remains relaxed. "Why do you think she'll kill you this time?"

I take another sip of tea as honesty manifests into tears, burning my eyes. "Because I'm not sure I want to fight her this time. I'm a weak, ugly girl who might as well listen to her."

Now Kelly gives me a disapproving stare. "You know better than to call yourself those things. Why do you listen to her?"

I shrug.

"Is it easier to fall back into bad habits rather than to fight them?"

Of course, it's easier to fall back into bad habits. Most

people don't understand eating disorders. They think they are a selfish cry for attention from entitled girls. But those people are wrong.

Imagine falling through the sky in a doomed aircraft with limbs paralyzed by fear, keeping you from jumping and pulling the parachute cord. That's what it feels like to have an eating disorder. You know how to save yourself, but you are unable to do so. Some think it's just as simple as to eat—pull the cord. But it's not.

Kelly opens the drawer beside her desk and retrieves a leather bound journal. She hands it to me then settles back in her chair. "I have a proposition."

I glide my fingers over the journal. Its thick, brown leather cover smells like a horse saddle. This isn't something she dug out of an old desk drawer or tore off a bookshelf. It's free of any dust, and the pages are crisp and white. Kelly bought this for me.

Clutching the journal tight against my stomach, I ask, "What are you proposing?"

She nods toward the gift. "Write about how you killed Anna the first time. Pour it all out. It's best to view an issue from all angles, and writing will enable you to do so. You might find something you'd not encounter otherwise."

I tighten my grip on the book. "I don't want to." I can't look her in the eyes. I really, truly, and seriously do not want to write about Anna.

"Maybe if you write about the agony Anna put you through, then you will have new insight into your current situation. You could find the strength to, as you say, 'kill her again.'" She gestures air quotes.

I try to hand the journal back to her, but she won't take it.

"Tell me what you want, Ariel."

I verbalize the first thing that comes to mind. "I want to stop eating. To feel the spaces between my ribs with my fingers. I want to feel the pain of hunger and to have the control that comes from listening to Anna." My eyes widen at my confession. Do I really want those things?

"No, Ariel. What do you *really* want?"

Kelly sees deeper than my weakness. I attempt to turn off the darkness inside my mind and wriggle toward the light. When I do, I find that the truth is simple. Not many girls my age are thinking in terms of life and death, but I must. "I want to live." I mean it. I want to live, and I'm scared to die. I'm not stupid. I know entertaining an eating disorder is as dangerous as playing with matches while fueling a car—but sometimes, it's the dangerous things that are the most difficult to resist.

"Anna was my friend," I say. This is partially true. She was my best friend, but also my worst enemy.

Kelly considers my internal struggle. "You see the world through kaleidoscope glasses, Ariel. It's easy for you to remember when your mom let you eat ice cream and Popsicles for breakfast, lunch, and dinner. But when you only think of that, you're blocking out memories of the fever that kept you bedridden. Which is why she was doing all she could to get you to eat. Anna is the same way. Take the glasses off. See her for the part she truly played in your life."

The darkness returns like I haven't pushed it away. "She was my friend," I argue. I flip the pages of the journal with my thumb. They are blank—not like the spiral-bound, college ruled notebooks that I use to take notes with in class. "I wouldn't know what to write about."

"Write about the good, the bad, and the ugly. Write about the end."

I consider her suggestion. I could argue that it was the hurricane that killed Anna, but that wouldn't be the full truth. She died by my hand. I remember that time in fragments, a lot like the colorful beads at the bottom of a kaleidoscope, little pieces that make a colorful picture—or a dizzying nightmare. Many people may think kaleidoscopes are for kids, but I love them. I collect them. There is something about the sound the beads make as they shift, the colors, and the images they create.

My relationship with Anna fell apart two weeks before Hurricane Irma tore through Florida in September of 2017.

Kelly looks at the clock. "Time's up for today. But I have one more question." She waits until I lift my eyes toward her. "What are you looking forward to in life? Do you have anything you can work toward?"

I don't have to think about an answer. "My driving test. I'm seventeen, but being sick kept me from accumulating hours. Mom says I can take the test in a few months." I can't express how much I would like the freedom that would come from having my driver's license.

"When you feel like giving up, think about how exciting it will be to pass the test. Sound good?"

I nod.

"We have an appointment scheduled for the same time next week. Does that work for you?"

I almost roll my eyes. Kelly and I have been having weekly dates at the same time every Tuesday since I got out of treatment. "Yes. I'll see you then."

Kelly walks me to the door. I still have the journal in my hands as I step over the threshold. When I turn to thank her, she's already closed the door.

SINCE DAD no longer lives with Mom and me, the house is quiet. I sit in my room, tired of re-watching shows on my tablet. I turn off my iPad and lie in bed, staring at the ceiling. My collection of kaleidoscopes sits on top of my bookshelf in the corner. I sit cross-legged and study them. My gaze lands on the journal I shoved between a copy of *Pride and Prejudice* and *The Selection*. I retrieve the journal and set it in my lap.

I remember the day when things started to go wrong. I guess I'll write a few things, a few pieces of that day . . .

Chapter 2

M onday, September 4th, 2017

Home

10:00 AM

It was Labor Day, so I slept in as long as I could. If my eyes had stayed closed, and if I had continued the REM cycle, then I could have avoided the appointment. The one I would have rather pretended didn't exist. When my eyes finally opened, I willed them to drift shut but couldn't force myself back to sleep. The day would have continued whether I slept in or rolled out of bed.

I braced myself by taking a quick intake of breath, then I threw the covers off and shivered at the chilled air. Mom kept the house at seventy-four degrees, but it felt like sixty. I wrapped my arms around myself and shuffled to the bathroom.

Anna's gaze met mine in the mirror. I found a discarded towel to stand on so my feet wouldn't touch the cold tile.

Here's the thing. People might think it sounds creepy to see someone in the mirror. But I wasn't, and have never been, schizophrenic.

When I raised my head and faced my reflection head on, there were two versions of myself. The ugly one and the beautiful one. Me and Anna. My skin bulged, but hers was flat against her stomach and hips. My brown hair lay limp and thin at my shoulders, but her lush, thick copper-brown locks fell in beachy waves across her shoulders. She also had boobs—cups size C. I would have been lucky to pull off a B.

If Anna and I were in a movie, she'd be the main character. Me? I'd probably be the lame BFF who gets killed by a stray bullet or is the first to disappear in a haunted house.

You see, I've always been harsh about my body. What sixteen-year-old isn't? It comes with the ever-present hormones that keep us in a constant state of PMS. I'm seventeen now and I still struggle with body image, but it was worse when I was sixteen.

Unfortunately, at that time in my life, I couldn't blame my self-judgment on PMS. I hadn't had my period in almost two years.

I hated the girl I saw in the mirror. I loved her. I *was* her.

"Morning," she said.

Instead of answering, I pulled my sleep shirt over my head, tossed it onto the floor, and searched the piles of laundry for a bra. Finding a lacy sky blue push-up, I wrapped it around my stomach, clipped it behind my back, and pulled it around my shoulders.

"What are you going to do?" She was referring to the appointment.

Later, at noon, I was scheduled to meet with the director of admissions and the nutritionist at Whole Healing Treatment, or WHT for short. I needed to prepare for my admittance which would take place in two days. I'd been to treatment before, but not to WHT. The last stint in treatment I'd had took place a year prior, in Jacksonville, Florida. But Mom found one closer to home in Orlando. At the meeting at noon, I was to confirm my admittance on Wednesday and go over details.

Footsteps came from the hallway. Mom poked her head into the bathroom without knocking. The night before, she'd told me that she wanted to go to the store to get water before the appointment. A hurricane in the Atlantic had Floridians beginning preparations, just in case the storm veered in our direction.

"Ariel, are you ready? I want to—" She stopped talking, probably caught off guard by the sight of my half-clothed body.

I scrambled for a T-shirt, hating that she saw me without one. I hated for anyone to see my body and find it disappointing.

I found a tank top, shoved my hands through the straps, and pulled it over my stomach.

Mom's eyes lingered longer than I would have liked. A crease formed between her brows, and her lips pinched together.

I hunched and crossed my arms over my stomach. "What?"

"It's worse than I thought," she whispered. She tilted her gaze to my face. "Ariel, you promised . . . you said . . . "

Let me pause here. The thing about eating disorders I understand now but didn't fully grasp then—is how much they steal. The worried look on Mom's face, and the anguish lilt of her voice are things I'll carry with me forever.

Believe me. I wanted to change for her, to be the daughter I once was—but despite that desire, I couldn't seem to give her what she wanted. And it burned guilt into my soul.

Labor Day is one of the days I remember most because of those five whispered words.

"It's worse than I thought."

The little girl in me went toward her. I wrapped my arms

around her, buried my head in her shoulder, and said, "I'm sorry."

And I was. I mean, I couldn't *force myself* to eat and gain weight and become healthy—but I'd wished to have the desire. For Mom's sake, at least. The white lies I had given her, such as, "I'm fine," and, "I'm doing better," were exposed as ghosts instead of truths as soon as she saw me in my bra and pajama bottoms.

Mom hugged me back. "What did I do wrong?"

I eased back. I never wanted her to think like that. "Mom, you didn't do anything wrong. It's me. I'm sorry. I don't know how to change. I—" I stopped myself before saying, "I don't want to change."

There is a very real yo-yo aspect to eating disorders. One moment, I wanted freedom from Anna's voice and the painful life she had brought with her—and then other times I wanted to staple Anna to my brain, my body, and keep her there forever. The same way Peter Pan had tried to attach his shadow to his body.

Mom wiped her cheeks and forced a smile. "It's all right. We're going to meet Hanna and Jennifer today. Only a few more days and you can start to get better."

I forced a smile. I knew that treatment could heal my body temporarily—like it did the time before. But my mind was filled with Anna. I wasn't ready to evict her yet.

"Get ready. We need to hurry. The store opened at ten, and we need to arrive early if we want to get water."

I searched the floor for more clothes. "I thought this hurricane wasn't supposed to come for another week."

"Forecasters are saying this is a big one. The Governor issued a state of emergency today. I don't want to lose my chance of getting water while there's still some left to buy."

My stomach flipped when she said, "big one." The last time we saw damage caused by a hurricane was the previous year when Matthew ripped up the east coast. Its impact damaged homes and forced many to evacuate to places like Orlando or Tampa in an effort to escape the storm's path.

"Okay, I'll be right there."

Mom left, and Anna cast me a worried look. "Fake sick so you can get out of the appointment."

I wish . . .

"Do it. Get yourself to throw up. Mom would believe that, and you'd be able to get rid of more calories. Win, win."

I slipped off my pajama bottoms and found a pair of jeans. It might be eighty degrees, but my body ran cold. *I wish I could, but Mom would drag me to the appointment.*

Anna huffed and gave me more solutions to my problem. "Take too long at the store and miss the appointment. Hide in the store. Break a bone, and go to the hospital for a cast instead of treatment."

But I couldn't do any of them. Anna's voice jumbled my brain with fearful thoughts. I was smart enough to know that, in the current situation, the only way out was through.

I met Mom in the kitchen. "Mind if I bring Mrs. Jevery the cookies I made for her before we go?"

She grabbed the keys. "If you're fast. Meet me in the car."

I scooped a plate of chocolate-and-peanut-butter-chip cookies off the counter, then I ran to the house next door.

I know it sounds strange that an anorexic girl would make cookies—but let me tell you, I could bake my butt off. I baked so much that I'd become known as the neighborhood's *free goodies princess.* At least, that's what Mrs. Jevery—who got the most of my goods—said.

I dashed up to her front porch and rang the doorbell.

The store

11:00 AM

People filled the warehouse club, causing me to wonder if we would be able to buy water. Were this many people stocking up on hurricane supplies, or simply taking advantage of their free time on Labor Day? If nothing else, I was grateful to have the distraction from my upcoming appointment.

Fluorescent lights reflected off the concrete floors, casting a white glare over everything. Oversized carts, which were pushed by frenzied shoppers, clattered by Mom and I as we wove our way toward the water aisle. I loved shopping. Mom and I went at least once a week when I assembled ingredients that I'd need for dinners and baked goods. Mom didn't mind that I cooked dinner more nights than not. This made certain I could eat only the foods I wanted.

A small boy ran into my leg. The force of him nearly knocked me over. I righted myself and set a hand on his head to steady us both. The throngs of people made it hard to separate one family from another, but before I could stoop to ask his name or where his family was, I heard a voice.

"Jason," a frantic female called.

I swiveled toward the sound. Mom stopped the cart. She'd picked one with a squeaky front wheel that alternated between screaming and swiveling at odd moments. I waved her on. "Go ahead, I'll catch up."

The woman waited for a cart to pass, then she crossed the divide toward the boy and me. She took his hand. "C'mon, honey, you can't run off like that." She looked at me. "Thank you."

"Sure. It was nothing." Jason could have run into anyone's leg. The haunting expression in her eyes, probably caused by the idea of losing her son, made me wonder—did my mom ever panic over losing me? The fear bulging in the woman's eyes reminded me of how Mom looked at me that morning.

Standing in the store amongst the other shoppers, I heard a voice for the first time. It was probably my own, but it was the first time that a pang in my heart accompanied it. *What would Mom do if you died?*

Died? The word struck me. I wouldn't die. I was sixteen, for gosh sake. But the seed had been planted.

I stepped into the stream of people and wove my way toward the back of the store. I found Mom in the water aisle line. She'd been right to come early. People filled their carts already. She and I hefted two cases of forty bottles each into the cart. Some people forced five or six cases into their carts. How big could their families be for them to have needed that much water? Before big storms approached, we would typically fill our bathtubs with water for non-drinking purposes.

Mom and I shuffled through rows of shelves that were stacked as high as small houses. We bought protein granola bars, crackers, low calorie popcorn, bread, peanut butter, cans of chicken noodle soup, charcoal, matches, and trail mix. We stocked up on toilet paper, garbage bags, vitamins, and anything else we thought we might need in bulk quantity. Our cart was nearly overflowing by the time we made it to the checkout line.

A sound of buzzing distracted me. I checked my phone, but it wasn't me. "Mom, is that your phone?"

She pulled hers out of her purse and flipped her thumb across the screen. "This is Connie." She plugged her other ear as she listened. "I'm sorry, can you repeat that?" She squinted at the floor with a frown as she listened. "Are you sure? Our appointment was for . . . I see. Yes, we'll make it work . . . Okay. See you then."

Was that the treatment facility canceling our meeting? I forced myself to remain calm, but inwardly I jumped and screamed in victory. "Who was that?" I said in the dullest, most disinterested voice I could muster.

"That was Jennifer. She asked if we could postpone until five today."

The hope in my chest deflated. "Oh." Not the cancellation I'd hoped for.

Mom tapped her manicured-but-unpolished nail on the cart handle. "We'll go to my mom's house for a bit."

"It's only eleven."

Her tap-tap-tapping picked up speed. "We—we'll figure it out."

GRANDMA'S HOUSE

12:00 PM

Did Mom expect us to sit here for five hours? Grandma sat on her old, ugly plaid couch in front of the TV. Mom sat beside her, while I relaxed in the reclining chair. I loved Grandma, but I'd rather be in my bedroom while awaiting the undesired appointment.

Grandma's house has always smelled like brownies and lemons. Weird combo, I know, but the scent uniquely captures who she is. She has the best double chocolate brownie recipe in existence, and she squeezes lemons into every glass of water she drinks. She says it's what has kept her alive so long. She also claims that chocolate is the key to longevity, but I'm not as sure. At almost eighty years of age, and still in as good of health as a forty year old, I think she has the right to say whatever she wants. But still—*chocolate*?

The voices that came from The Weather Channel filled the room, and my phone vibrated with a text. Yes, something to occupy my mind. I tuned out everything else and checked my screen.

JAX: *Meet me at the park tonight?*

·   ·   ·

I STILL STUMBLED over calling him my boyfriend, and I couldn't believe how lucky I was to have him. We had been friends since elementary school. He used to live in my neighborhood— before we moved to a nicer one. He played on both the basketball and the baseball teams. His breakup with Hadley, the swimming teams' freestyle star, made the rounds at school recently. At times, I couldn't help but wonder, was I his rebound girl? But I knew Jax wasn't like that. He and I had always had a connection. It seemed natural for us to date after so many years of friendship. The fact that he broke up with Hadley had nothing to do with us. I hoped not, at least.

ME: *The park?*

WE'D NEVER MET at a park before. What could he have been referring to?

JAX: *The one at the end of your street. You have your appointment today, right? Tell me about it in person.*

THE STUPID APPOINTMENT was tainting everything. What would Jax and I do when I went to treatment? Would he still want to be my boyfriend afterwards, or would he find someone else while I was trapped?

ME: *Yes. Appt. has been rescheduled to 5. I'm not sure my mom will let me out at night.*
 Jax: *Wanna sneak out?*

· · ·

I CHECKED to see if Mom or Grandma were looking. Both seemed fixated on the TV.

ME: *You know I'm not that kind of girl. But, why not?*
    Jax: *I don't want to get you into trouble or force you to do it if you'd be uncomfortable. But I do really want to see you.*
    Me: *I want to see you too.*
    Jax: *XoXo*
    Me: *XoXoXoXoXoXo*
    Jax: *Haha, this could go on forever. Meet you at ten?*
    Me: *See you then. <3*

THE ATTENTION JAX showered me with gave me validation. It made me believe I could be worth something to someone.

Okay, so admitting that probably makes me seem shallow—but I'm sure most girls can relate. There's something inside of us that comes alive when a boy likes us and gives us affection. Well it does to me, at least.

Hope texted me as I finished texting Jax. Hope was the only girl who still spoke to me—besides Anna, of course. This couldn't be better timing. I was desperate for the distraction.

HOPE: *I need to talk to youuuuuuu!*

I GRINNED.
    "Ariel?"
    I started to thumb a response to Hope.

ME: *I have an appointment . . .*

. . .

"Ariel?"

I jerked my head in the direction of the voice. Mom gave me a pointed look. Grandma held the remote in one hand and pointed it at the TV, turning down the volume.

"Yes?"

"Your grandma asked you how school's going," Mom said.

"School's fine. It's nice to have today off. Maybe we'll get more time off if—" I gestured toward the TV "—if the hurricane comes closer."

Last year, when Hurricane Andrew scared the west coast, schools all the way to Tampa decided to close. I loved not having school, but I didn't want any more time away from Jax before treatment.

Grandma slapped the remote on the couch beside her and gave a laugh. "I've lived through many hurricanes. It could go out to sea. Forecasters can't predict a storm like this one. I've seen them go all sorts of directions. But you might be right about school." She pointed a wrinkled finger at me, her short, curly gray hair framing her face. "Lucky you, eh?" She winked. "It's your junior year. You already took those STDs, right? You're applying to colleges?"

I coughed to keep from laughing. Mom pinched her lips to suppress a smile. "SATs," I corrected her. "And no, I won't apply until next year. My boyfriend, Jax, is a senior, and starts dual enrollment with the community college next semester." Maybe I shouldn't have said Jax's name in the same conversation as STDs.

The images on TV distracted Grandma from our conversation. She turned the volume up again. Spaghetti lines of the hurricane's projected path filled the screen. A blur of lines covered the east coast side of the state, but nothing touched the middle or the Gulf Coast.

"See?" Grandma said. "Nothing to worry about."

The name of the hurricane was displayed beneath the images.

Irma.

Home

1:30 PM

Mom decided we should return home instead of spending the whole afternoon with Grandma, waiting for my appointment. I stood in the kitchen, mixing a batch of brownies, when the front door whooshed open and Hope entered.

"When you didn't answer my text, I figured I'd just come over," she said.

I should have known. Whereas Anna would be the main character in any movie, Hope has always been the smart and solid friend—someone you can go to for advice or adventure. Think Flounder from *The Little Mermaid* or Pascal from *Tangled*. Yes, I know I just referred to my only friend as an animal—but let's be real. Those animals had big roles.

The continuous stirring motion burned the muscles of my arm, but I preferred to do that rather than use a hand-held mixer. Something as simple as mixing brownie batter burned calories, so I wanted to burn as many as I could. Hope's unannounced arrival set me on edge like any divergence from the controlled structure of my life. "You didn't have to come."

Hope tossed a strand of shimmery, black hair over her shoulder and closed the door behind her. She's always looked more like her Puerto Rican mom than her German dad. "What does it matter? I'm here now."

I shrugged and turned back to mixing. The scent of chocolate made my mouth water. My brain demanded that I stick my finger in the bowl and lick the chocolate, but Anna—the dark presence inside of me—latched onto any weakness in my brain and forced the desire to flee. A constant battle warred within me, and I couldn't choose a side. Baking and cooking were a substitute for eating. I may not physically eat all the cookies, muffins, brownies, cakes, and pies I made, but I devoured them with my eyes. That would have to be enough.

Hope's disappointed voice made me freeze. "Do you want me to leave?"

She must have caught on to my unwelcoming attitude. "No, it's not that." My relationship with Hope was like the one I had with my mom. I wanted to let her in. I had an urge to share with her the hateful things Anna whispered in my ears. I wanted to ask her to help me—but I couldn't. Anna prevented me from voicing my pain, as well as my desperation for freedom, to anyone who could help.

"I'm not giving up on you, Ariel," Hope said.

Part of me wished she would move on like my other friends, but a deeper part of me wanted her to keep pushing until she broke down my walls. "I'm not sure I'm worth hanging onto."

Hope plopped down onto a stool at the kitchen island. "Your appointment is today, right?"

I banged the whisk on the side of the bowl, then tossed it into the sink. I didn't finish my text earlier. "How did you know?"

"I asked your mom. You don't ever tell me anything, so . . ." She gave me an opportunity to apologize, but I didn't.

"Yes," I said. "The appointment is in a few hours."

She set her arms on the white granite countertop. "Are you scared?"

I reached for a glass baking dish under one of the kitchen counters. The weight of it made me lose my balance. I gripped the counter to steady myself, hoping Hope didn't notice. She did.

"When are you being admitted?"

The glass dish clanked against the granite as I set it on the counter. "Wednesday."

"I'm glad."

Anger rose in my chest like a cresting wave, and I clenched my teeth to keep from yelling. Instead, I pulled the cooking spray from a cupboard. A film of olive oil coated a section of counter as I sprayed the dish. "Do you want me to bring you some of these?" I dumped the brownie mix into the dish. Maybe changing the subject would help me to regain mental and emotional equilibrium.

"Yeah, they look great."

Lines of batter marred the bowl as I used a rubber spatula to scrap it into the baking dish. Again, I had the urge to stick my finger in for a taste. I would cut a few bars for Hope and her boyfriend, Clark, and then bring the rest of the brownies to Jax's lunch table. I wasn't close with his friends, but they loved it when I brought desserts.

When I didn't respond, Hope stood and leaned against the counter. "Do you want me to go?"

Want? The only thing I *wanted* was to feel beautiful—to have emptiness in my stomach and pride at reaching my goal. I didn't want anything else, and I didn't have the energy for anything else, either. Sleeping, or watching TV, would be just fine for me.

Hope must have picked up on my unspoken "yes." She said, "I'll leave for today, but I'll keep coming back."

"I'm sorry. I'm just . . . not feeling great today."

"Because of the appointment?"

I shrugged. I was never okay, but the appointment took up most of my thoughts.

"It'll be fine. You'll see. Treatment will stick this time. I can visit if you'd let me."

The word *stick* made me cringe. Stick like the fat on my love handles? I shoved the dish in the oven and set the timer. "Can we not talk about this?"

Hope rounded the counter and squeezed me in a hug. "I want my friend back. I love you." I could smell her fruity breath mint and the unique scent that she always seemed to carry. You know the smell when you walk into your best friend's house, the one that captures who she is? Hope's scent felt like home, and I found myself hugging her back. Her solid presence did something to my heart—but I didn't want to hurt Anna, so I let go.

When Hope pulled away, she wiped a tear from her eye. "See you tomorrow. Let me know how the appointment goes, okay?"

"Sure."

Her smile wavered as she turned. We both knew I wouldn't fill her in later today, but I couldn't shake the feeling that she loved me anyway.

W*HOLE* H*EALING* T*REATMENT* Facility
5:00 PM

Hanna, the nutritionist—and Jennifer, the admissions counselor—sat in black, striped-accented chairs while Mom and I sat on a white couch in the belly of the treatment facility. Before the meeting, they made me put on a hospital gown and shiver my way to a scale. They forced me to stand backwards on the scale while they documented my weight. By the time I had my clothes back on I was cold enough to turn a hot tub's temperature lukewarm.

Jennifer consulted the clipboard that was balanced atop her crossed legs. "I wish we could get you in sooner, but our earliest opening is Wednesday in the early evening. I'd advise you to admit yourself into the hospital until then and start refeeding. Your vitals are dangerously low."

"No," I said before Mom could respond.

Hanna used a warm but patronizing voice. "What have you eaten today, honey?" The way she said it suggested she already knew the answer.

I turned my gaze to the floor and didn't answer.

Mom played with the zipper on her purse. "You can't make room? It's only two days."

Jennifer clicked her pen. "I wish we could, but the soonest we could get her in is on Wednesday. We have a resident who is being discharged."

"And you think she needs to be in the hospital?" Mom asked.

Hanna answered this time. "Unless she can eat three meals a day, then yes. But even if she did that, I would still advise the hospital. They can monitor her and make sure she's getting proper nutrition and care."

"I can eat," I said. "I'll eat. I'm not going to the hospital."

Everyone looked at me.

"I'll eat. I promise." The thought of being force-fed with a tube scared me more than the idea of choosing my own meals at home.

"I don't think—"

"No, Mom," I interrupted. I mean it. I'll eat."

Hanna looked back and forth between us. "I can write a customized meal plan for you to follow for the next two days. I still think the hospital would be a better idea, but we can't force you to go, especially if neither of you agree to it."

I could *not* go to the hospital. If I was admitted today, then I wouldn't have a chance to see Jax—and I absolutely had to see him before I went.

Mom and I locked eyes, and she seemed to have read the determination on my expression. She'd have to drag me into the hospital fighting and crying before I would be admitted. I would not go willingly.

"Can we look at the meal plan?" Mom said.

Hanna left the room to gather paperwork.

"If you experience anything out of the ordinary, then I suggest you go to the hospital," Jennifer said.

I forced an earnest, yet concerned, expression and nodded in agreement. Did the seriousness of the situation scare me? Of course! As I sat in that counseling room two days before I was to be admitted, I was terrified that I might die. The old, healthy, Ariel wanted to run to the hospital—but Anna kept me from taking Hanna and Jennifer's concern seriously.

I know it sounds crazy. Why would I *willingly* choose to die rather than get help? But that's what I'm trying to explain and understand for myself too. Eating disorders are not rational. They make no sense from the outside looking in. But when I was in the middle of it—and even now, as I contemplate if it's worth fighting—there is this attraction I have to Anna, my eating disorder. It's like a first love you never get over.

Hanna came back and talked with me about my relationship with food. She wrote guidelines for what I should be eating over the next few days. The calorie count would max that of a Hobbit who ate a second, third, and fourth breakfast. I'd look like a whale if I followed her directions, but I had no choice but to agree. I'd eat a little more. I didn't want to die, but I also couldn't be as sick as they were making me out to be.

Before we left, both women told Mom to call them if she had any concerns, and they told me they'd see me in two days.

In the parking lot, Mom and I shut ourselves in the car. Mom gripped the steering wheel and stared straight ahead, unmoving.

"Mom?"

She didn't flinch.

"Mom?"

Finally, she jerked toward me.

"Are you okay?"

The engine came to life as she started the car. "I hope I'm making the right choice. If anything happens to you . . ."

"It won't, Mom. I promise. I'm okay. I'll follow the meal plan. I've done it before. It's better than going to the hospital."

"But if you were in the hospital, I'd know that you were safe. If something happens to you, I would never forgive myself."

"I'm okay. Please understand that."

With a sigh, Mom backed out of the parking space and didn't even cast me a glance. I hated that I'd caused her this burden, but I didn't know what else to do. The only thing that would ease her fears was for me to eat. The thought of moving from my safe foods scared the crap out of me—but what choice did I have? Both Hanna's and Jennifer's concern scared me enough to want to eat just a *little* more. But only a little. I wanted to live. Isn't that what we all want? But not all people have to make the choice.

I did.

I still do.

But I'm just not sure that I'm strong enough.

THE PARK

10:00 PM

Sneaking out of the house was easier than it should have been. Since I was a model sixteen year old and didn't give my parents a reason to worry about me, I had no trouble shimmying out of my ground-floor window and walking down the street toward the park.

I saw a form sitting on a swing. "Jax," I whispered. Because we'd been friends for so long, I could recognize his silhouette even in the dark.

The swing squeaked as he stood and took the last few steps toward me. He hugged me around the waist and spun me around. "I missed you," he said into my neck. His warm breath gave me the good kind of shivers, not the cold ones that made me want to hibernate like a black bear.

"I missed you too. Are we lame? It's only been two days since we saw each other."

He pulled back and looked at me, shadows obscuring his features. "I know."

"What are you thinking?" The way he studied me made me worry he might not like the way I looked. I wished Mom wouldn't have made me eat dinner. I told Anna I'd do sit-ups when I got home to burn off the calories.

"I was thinking about how we used to sneak out as kids. But this is better, because we get to do this." He leaned in and gave me a chocolate-melting kiss. It tasted better than candy, and trust me, I love me some chocolate. Or I used to, before Anna.

When he let go, I couldn't help but giggle. "Technically, we could have done that when we were kids, but exchanging saliva with a boy was the last thing on my to-do list at that age."

"I'm glad we grew up, then," he said. Then he filled the distance between our lips again. I tried not to cringe when his hand rested on my hip. "Come on." He tugged me toward the swings.

I settled on one of the rubber seats, and Jax stood behind me to push. I leaned back and let my feet walk the sky each time I swung forward. Jax's hands on my back pushing me forward almost meant more to me than his kisses. He wasn't the type of boy to mess with a girl, which is why I found his breakup with Hadley perplexing, especially when she was attractive and I was not. His hands propelled me onward, and I knew I was special to him. I meant something to him.

Jax was the type of boy who bought his single mom flowers on Valentine's Day and drove his middle-school-aged brother to baseball practice so his mom could work sixty-hour weeks. His hands prepared meals, fixed broken electronics, washed dishes, folded laundry, and then he took the time to push me on a park swing.

I soared.

When the swing slowed, Jax waited behind me on the grass. His presence held me solid against the earth. He was one of the only aspects of my life that was not completely touched by Anna. I wanted to be the best girl I could be for him.

"How did your appointment go?"

If it wasn't for his gentle hands that held me in place, I probably would've ran. I didn't want to think about the things I'd have to eat in treatment. But Jennifer's dire suggestion that I admit myself into a hospital stuck to my brain like spilled, sugary juice left to dry on hardwood floors. The thought hardened to my mind the more it sat, and panic made me second-guess my decision to try and eat on my own. What if I died? Would it be painful, or would my heart stop beating one moment and my life fade away the next moment?

Dizziness clouded my vision like static on an old TV. I stumbled to the playset. I heard Jax's footfalls in the woodchips behind me as I walked up the steps toward one of the towers. As I reached the top, I had to stop and grip one of the railings to keep from falling. Jax reached me and wrapped his arm around my waist. He guided me to the floor of the structure. His breathing quickened. His movements were a blur, but I could tell he was tapping a code into his phone to unlock it.

"Stop," I said. "I'm okay."

He had already dialed *9-1*, and his thumb hovered over the second *1*.

"You're okay?"

This wasn't right. None of it was. I recognized that I was being stupid. This was my second major bad decision of the day. My first was not admitting myself into the hospital, and the second was not allowing Jax to call for help. And that bothered me. I realized I was the worst kind of high-maintenance girlfriend. I didn't plan on it. Anna didn't tell me I'd alienate my family and friends if I followed her path, but now I was so deep inside her patterns that I couldn't shake free, and now those I loved were coming down with me.

The honest truth scares me as I write this. My letters are sloppy. If Kelly reads this at my next appointment, she might ask me to read it to her. Only the one who wrote with shaking hands and teary eyes can decipher something this messy.

Because the truth is—I loved Jax. But I loved Anna more. I hate writing those words. I want to cross them out. I hate the truth. Why haven't I noticed it before now? I knew I was hurting Jax by not being the best version of myself, but Anna convinced me it was okay, that *I* was okay.

But I wasn't.

I remember clutching the front of this T-shirt as I regained my breath. He smelled like guy. Not the locker room, sweaty, or over cologned kind of guy. Instead, he smelled like the kind of guy who slept in sheets laundered with fresh detergent, used manly bars of soap, and washed dishes with orange scented dish soap. "I'll be okay." I held his wrist, then set his phone on the fake wood of the playset.

"Are you sure?"

I nodded against his chest.

"What did they say at your appointment? Are you leaving?" The eagerness in his tone suggested he wanted me to leave. At the time I bristled in offense, but now my heart breaks a little to know he loved me enough to let me go.

A car drove by the playground, and we watched its taillights fade around a corner.

"I'll leave on Wednesday."

His arm tightened around my waist. "For sure?"

"Yep." I considered leaving out the part about the hospital, but I knew it'd be best to tell him.

"Why didn't you go?"

I still leaned against Jax. I wanted to memorize this moment, because I knew I would soon be lying in bed at treatment and wishing I was anywhere else. I admitted to Jax what I'd only thus admitted to myself. "I'm scared."

"Of the hospital?"

"Of eating."

His arm loosened. "I don't get that."

"I know."

"I want to help."

"You can't."

"Why?"

"Because there's nothing you can do."

He groaned in frustration. "There has to be something."

My teeth clenched into my bottom lip. "Just don't stop."

"Stop what?"

"Trying."

He leaned in and planted a sweet kiss on my forehead. "I won't. But I'm scared for you. What if . . ."

I knew what it was that he couldn't seem to say.

What if I died?

And this is the question that has me writing in this journal. Only now the question is a bit more complex.

Do I have the strength to fight off death again—and do I even want to?

Five months ago, we sat in silence, staring across the dark playground, not aware of the pain that was ahead of us. He tried to lighten the mood. "Do you want to hang out with me after school tomorrow? I can take you out for coffee. It might be the last date we can fit in before Wednesday."

Jax had been trying to get me to go on a coffee date for weeks. I enjoyed sitting in his car and listening to music, but the boy in him wanted to bring me somewhere. Coffee shops weren't that bad. I could easily order herbal tea or straight black coffee and not consume a single calorie. But sometimes the simple act of looking at the cookies and muffins behind the glass gave me anxiety. I wanted to eat them, but I wouldn't let myself. Avoiding the situation altogether was ideal.

But then again, I wanted to spend time with him, so I couldn't decline. "Yes." The roar of another car sounded in the distance. I watched as the car passed the park. "I should probably get home before Mom notices I'm gone."

He stood. "I don't want to get you in trouble."

"Don't worry, you won't."

He walked me down the playset, his thumb hooked in the loop of my jeans to keep me steady, then led me across the park. He came to a halt at a spot where my house was in view. "I'll wait here until you text me that you're inside."

"I'll be fine walking home alone."

"I know, but I want to make sure you're safe."

How did I end up with a guy like him? A lot of guys grabbed girls' backsides as they walked down the halls, texted lewd messages to them, peppered their conversations with innuendoes, or openly cheated on them—but somehow, I ended up with the alien species of high school boy.

He gave me a quick kiss then released my hand to let me walk away.

BEDROOM

11:00 PM

I stood in front of the bathroom mirror for a long time that night as Anna and I argued.

I should go to the hospital.

"Why?"

Because Jennifer said I should, and she sees girls like me every day. If she's worried, then I'm probably in real danger.

"You ate a lot for dinner. I'm sure you're fine."

She was right. I hadn't eaten that much in days. My stomach

cramped in pain, and I swallowed a moment of panic. Food had entered my mouth, my stomach, and soon it would add inches to my thighs. I was stupid for losing control.

"You shouldn't have eaten so much. If you keep at it, you'll become even more unattractive than you already are."

I know.

"Then do something about it."

But Jennifer said—ugh. I don't know what to do.

"Weigh yourself."

I pulled the scale out from beneath the sink. Unwilling to weight myself unless I was naked, I stripped and stepped onto the digital scale. The sleek metal shocked the soles of my feet with cold. As soon as the digital numbers appeared, I considered punching the mirror.

"I told you not to lose control," Anna said.

The scale told me that I was a half-pound higher than I was yesterday.

If there is anyone who is reading this journal and thinks I was being unreasonable, you might be right. But voices like Anna aren't reasonable, and I couldn't turn her off like a light switch.

Do you ever hear that negative voice inside of your head when you look in the mirror, eat an extra brownie, or take the elevator instead of the stairs? That's what Anna's voice was— and is—to me. Her presence didn't make me crazy, but I had listened to her so many times that I didn't know how to stop. When I tried to make a decision that went against hers, the panic that would follow made me want to hide in my room. I literally couldn't control myself.

Now I'm not sure if I can fight her again. Her voice has always been strong, and we built habits together. Habits that I've tried to end—but it's only been five months. Is five months long enough to keep her away?

How much longer do I have to fight?

Chapter 3

Present
    January 17th, 2018

THE SKY blue bra with a lace back doesn't fit anymore. I'm too large now. I should consider this to be a good thing, because what girl doesn't want a bigger chest? But like the jeans that no longer fit me, this too-tight bra signifies a part of my past. *Skinny me* is gone.

I've seen Kelly twice since I started writing in the journal. Two weeks is a long time to write fragments of a day, but I remember parts of that week vividly. The reason might be the same as to why we remember the endings of books or movies more than the beginning. The week of Hurricane Irma marked the end of me and Anna.

At least, that's what I thought.

I unhook the blue bra and bury it beneath a pair of socks in my top dresser drawer. Maybe it will fit me again someday. But what would that mean?

"It would mean you were hot again. Because, girl, you have

gained." Anna's voice returns to my mind, but I don't push it away like I've been doing. I'm tired, and fighting her takes more effort than I'm willing to give. I want to rest, sleep, dream—or give up altogether.

Anna's voice sounds like my own voice, but there's a bite to her tone. Her voice is marked with hatred, longing, and perfection. I've talked to Kelly about how my eating disorder feels like a scene from a cheesy movie, one that shows a character who has an angel on one shoulder and a demon on the other. I preach kindness from one of my shoulders, but then I shout ugly things at myself from the other. They're in conflict with each other. The angry, sad, and abandoned voice starts to yell louder, and the reasonable, caring, and patient voice grows dimmer.

I find a black silk bra, put it on, and run my fingers over the sleek fabric. Nice bras come in larger sizes, as do pants—but it's the principle of them, not their existence, which bothers me. Do I want the black bra or the blue one? The angel or the demon? Health or the eating disorder?

This is my dilemma.

The journal rests on my nightstand. A pen serves as a book-mark, sticking out between the pages. I've written more than I thought I would, and the words have done something strange to me. I thought I'd hate writing about the end—but I actually like it. I want to write more, but I'm hesitant. The next part played out like a teenage drama. I hate drama. Unless, of course, it's on TV.

If I am to write about the events that led to my murdering Anna, then I must write about Tuesday. About Jax. About *another* ending.

I look away from the journal. Will writing any of this help the way Kelly seems to think? Will I find clarity as I write the end? Will I gather the will to keep fighting?

Or will I find that I'd rather give up?

I know what it'd require to end the fight. My body hasn't fully healed yet—that much is obvious. The lack of my period, after five months of recovery, is proof enough. My body hasn't finished gaining weight or restoring the functions of health that I once took for granted. I know for sure that my mind hasn't healed yet, either, because I can still hear Anna's voice.

But I had hoped my body would have at least caught up by now.

Anorexia is not a game. It's not a diet or a fad. It's life or death. It might seem strange for a seventeen year old to seriously consider death. I've never been suicidal, but anorexia is a slow type of death. It's a tug-of-war with the mind, soul, and body, and I'm not sure I can keep up the fight. I've met women who've had eating disorders for twenty, thirty, or forty years. The thought makes me want to sleep forever. Did they fight hard or give up?

And then there's the girl from treatment who died. Yes. *Died*. Two months after she was discharged, her heart stopped beating. Anorexia is a killer, I know this, but I'm not sure I'm strong enough to fight death. How many times can I kill a killer?

I check the time and scramble to find a shirt. I'll be late for school if I don't hurry. Hope expects for me to bring cookies, and I haven't bagged them yet. At least she's still with me even though others have left. I regret the Tuesday before the hurricane because it led to the loss of a relationship—one that I can't stop thinking about.

What would have happened if I'd done things differently?

Chapter 4

T uesday, *September 5th, 2017*

6:55 PM

I cocooned two brownies in plastic wrap for Hope and Clark, then placed the rest on a paper plate and covered it with the same wrap for Jax and his friends.

Mom walked into the kitchen and smiled at my preparations. "Can I make you some breakfast?"

The fitness models I'd scrolled through pictures of on Instagram earlier that morning had serious self-discipline in order to achieve their perfect bodies. "No, thanks. I'll get something myself." I chose the foods I ate with special care and strove to have the same self-control of the models in magazines, and actresses in online interviews.

I opened the fridge and pulled out an apple and a carton of yogurt. The night before, I had stayed awake for an hour planning what I would bring to school before I finally went to sleep. I had decided on these snacks.

Not only that, but I already had dinner planned too. Every food that passed through—or even touched—my lips baked in my mind like a casserole before I allowed myself to eat it. I counted the calories in my head again, hoping they'd be few enough to force the numbers on the scale to go down by bedtime.

I placed the food in my backpack with the wrapped brownies and carried the plate.

Mom gave me a hug, and I opened the door to make my way to the bus stop. "I'll make dinner tonight. Don't worry about it, okay?"

Fear paralyzed me. If she made dinner, I wouldn't have control over the calories. "What are you making?"

"I'm not sure yet, why?"

"I can make dinner. You know I like to."

She brushed brownie crumbs into the sink with her palm. "I know, but after the appointment yesterday I think I should make it. You've been limiting yourself. You know you need to gain weight. I'd hate myself if something happened to you and I could've done something."

I reached for her hand and gripped it the same way she used to take mine. "What happens to me is not your fault." I couldn't let her know how much her fear scared me.

"I'm your mother. I'm supposed to protect you. Speaking of which, why don't you stay home today and lie low?"

I took a step away, my hand still in hers. "No, Mom. Today and tomorrow are my last days with Jax and Hope before I go into treatment."

Moisture filled her eyes. "Text me every few hours so I know you're okay."

"I will. Jax is bringing me home, okay? We're going out for coffee after school."

Mom wiped under her eyes as optimism lit up her face. "You are?"

"If it's okay."

"I think it's a great idea. But . . . are you sure you don't want to stay home?"

I released her hand. "Yes."

She looked like she wanted to drag me to my room and lock me inside, but I knew she was trying to do what was best for me. She didn't know if she should keep me or let me go. She could have forced me to stay home—or even go to the hospital—but she knew she'd have to physically drag me there, and neither of us wanted that. I was that irrational.

I could tell that her brave smile was forced. "Okay. But take this." She unzipped my backpack, then pulled a peanut butter and jelly sandwich out of the fridge. "I made this for you last night. Eat it for lunch. If you won't let me bring you to the hospital, then I at least need to know you're eating. You promised to take care of yourself."

I didn't argue.

"You can throw the sandwich away at school. She'll never know," Anna said.

But I promised. And look how scared she is.

"So you want to eat it, but *can* you?"

I'd gotten to the point where eating actually caused me pain. You'd think anorexic girls were hungry all the time, but after not eating for so long, your stomach eventually stops hurting. The physical act of eating was more painful for me than hunger. At treatment, they would make me eat until I couldn't eat any more, then they would make me drink a meal replacement smoothie if I couldn't finish my meals. If I was *really* unlucky, then they'd feed me with a tube that would go through my nose and down my throat.

Could I eat?

I don't know.

"Ariel."

Mom waved her hand in front of my face, jolting me out of my argument with Anna. "You'll be late for the bus."

Hope's locker

8:45 AM

Hope gave me a once-over. "Need my sweater?"

I rubbed my arms, trying to warm them. The vents on the ceiling pushed cold air into the hallways. I curled my hands, which were already cold, into fists in effort to stay warm. The school was never warm enough. I should have had a cup of black coffee earlier—or at least green tea—to warm myself.

"You have one?" Unlike me, Hope was always hot. Why did she have a sweater?

She reached into her locker and extracted a hoodie. I couldn't reach for it fast enough.

Revelation dawned on me as I pulled the hoodie over my head. Hope didn't bring the sweater for her sake. She brought it for me.

This gesture proved even more that she was nothing like the other girls—those who ditched me during freshman year. She clung to me like peanut butter on the roof of my mouth, nourishing and persistent.

"Thanks. If you come to my locker, I can give you the brownies."

"I'll grab them at lunch. How did your appointment go?"

Since she was my best friend, I wanted to tell her about Jennifer's concern and how she suggested that I admit myself to the hospital, but I didn't know how to bring it up. "The appointment went fine. I'm going tomorrow after school."

"I can write letters and call, right?"

"Yeah."

She gave me a quick hug, then eased back, her hands

remaining on my shoulders as she said, "I'll miss you. But I'm glad you're getting help."

Why did everyone have to be so happy about my departure? I certainly wasn't. "It's not my choice."

She tilted her head. "You don't want to go?"

I shoved my hands in the front pocket of the hoodie and took a step back. "No." The idea that I'd have no control over the food that entered my body made me clench my hands into fists.

Her gaze traveled up and down my body again. "You need this. I want my friend back."

"I'm still your friend."

"I want the friend who hung out after school and came over for sleepovers." She gestured toward me. "Not this girl who hides in her kitchen baking things she doesn't eat. I want Ariel back. The Ariel who will go to the movies, a dinner date, or youth group with me.

Rumors used to circulate school about Hope—how being a pastor's kid caused her to be a religious snob. That sort of thing. But she expelled those rumors when she attended home-coming in a red, strapless dress, one that had the boys drooling. After that, people no longer saw her as a pastor's kid; instead, they saw her as a hottie. Some of the boys still referred to her as Red Dress Girl. They only cared enough to know her status on the hotness scale rather than her actual name.

Hope did nothing to encourage or to discourage the rumors. She didn't care what other people thought or didn't think about her. I always looked up to her for that.

I, on the other hand, seemed to lack that kind of strength.

"Hey." Clark, Hope's boyfriend—who coincidentally resembled the character Clark Kent from *Super-Man*—tiptoed behind Hope and squeezed her sides, tickling her. She screeched, almost dropping her phone as she spun around. "Don't do that when I'm talking to people."

He slid his glasses up the bridge of his nose. "But it's Ariel."

"So? Don't worry, I'll give you attention later."

"Have you seen Jax?" I asked Clark. Both Clark and Jax were seniors.

"Yeah, we just had class. I'm not sure where he is now though."

I checked my phone. There weren't any new texts from him.

ME: *Where are you?*

Jax: *Sorry. Got hung up talking about extra credit. See you at lunch.*

I SHOVED my phone into my pocket as the bell rang. Soon, the hallway became a traffic jam of students who scrambled toward their next class. I left Hope at her locker talking with Clark, and I joined the flow, disappointed that I couldn't see Jax. I wanted to be with him as much as possible before school ended the next day.

For once, lunchtime couldn't come fast enough. I pushed out of my mind thoughts about my mom and her mystery dinner. Or I tried, at least.

I'll admit—I ended up worrying more about food during my next class instead of daydreaming about Jax.

LUNCHROOM

12:00 PM

I balanced the plate of brownies on my forearm and grabbed the apple out of my backpack. The taste and texture of biting into a brownie filled my imagination as the scent of chocolate seeped through the plastic covering. The idea of sinking my teeth into a soft baked brownie and crunching on a

chocolate chip made my mouth water. It should be a require-
ment to always include chocolate chips in brownies. My fantasy
burst as my fingers brushed the plastic wrap of the PB&J while
I retrieved the apple.

"Don't eat it. You know how many calories there is in
peanut butter."

But—

"Stop being weak, or you'll be ugly forever."

Grinding my teeth, I dropped the sandwich bag and took
the apple only. Apples could take a while to eat if you took bites
that were small enough. I didn't need to feel guilty for eating
them, either. Anna approved.

But what I *really* wanted was a brownie.

The thought caused tension to increase in my head. I
decided to walk to the lunchroom, set the brownies on the
table, and allow others to snatch them up. If there were none
left—and there hardly ever were—then I wouldn't be tempted
anymore. Simple.

Cold air swirled around me as I walked toward the lunchroom. How did my classmates stay warm? How could the
school get by with keeping the temperature so low? Attending
was like slowly dying of frostbite.

I scanned the cafeteria and found the section of tables
where Jax sat. His group of friends watched me during lunch
like I was an interesting science experiment or the star a reality
TV show. An anorexic girl eating—fascinating.

Finally, toward the left side of the large room, I spotted him.
Jax. The boy who made me feel beautiful simply because of his
kindness. He sat at a round table that was surrounded by his
friends. From my point of view, I could see his profile. Jax's light
brown hair was trimmed on the sides and longer on top. He
wore a pair of khaki cargo shorts and a kale green T-shirt.

I made my way toward his table. As I approached, he
looked at me, and my breath caught in my throat as if I had

swallowed a large marshmallow. Seeing him under the fluorescent lights reminded me of the moonlight against his silhouette the night before. And the way he'd looked at me with concern.

He scooted off his chair, smiled, and walked toward me. Jax had one of those too-big smiles that showed part of his gums, but in an adorable way.

Jax looked at me in a way that made me blush. I knew, simply from that look, that I could've eaten a whole dozen cookies and he *still* would've thought I was gorgeous. Well, that might be a stretch, but I was euphoric at the way he watched me. I loved it. I was scared of it. What if treatment broke us apart?

His hands found my arms as I came to stop in front of him. He kissed my forehead then took the plate of brownies from me. "These look great. You didn't tell me you were bringing brownies when I saw you last night."

"I forgot."

He pulled me into a gentle hug. The folds of his shirt scrunched against my face, and I thought I caught a whiff of watermelon-flavored Jolly Ranchers. He probably didn't *really* smell like candy, but the idea of candy sounded amazing. I wanted something sugary, and simple things—like the smell of Jax— molded into my desires.

"I saved you a seat," he said, releasing me.

I sat and took a bite into my apple, enjoying the closeness of him.

"Is that all your eating?" A girl across the table from me said.

I halted my hand halfway to my mouth for another bite of apple. How was I supposed to respond? Was she judging me, or was she simply curious?

"My mom made me a huge breakfast," I lied. "I'm not very hungry."

She cast a wistful look. "I wish my mom made me big breakfasts."

A chorus of agreement ping-ponged around the table.

Jax unfolded the brownies' plastic wrap and slid the plate to the center of the table. Girls and guys reached for the chocolate, eager to claim the largest one. A girl with black hair and a nose ring slapped a big guy's hand away from the one she wanted. "Back off. This will totally ruin my diet, but I don't give a crap, I am *so* eating this."

In less than sixty seconds, there were only two brownies left. Jax pulled the tray back toward us as I continued to munch on my apple. *No, no, no.* They were all supposed to be gone.

"Thanks, Ariel," the girl with the nose ring said. I couldn't keep track of the faces as the students around the table echoed her.

Jax grabbed one of the last two brownies and took a bite. He pushed the tray toward me, gesturing toward the last one. "Want it?"

Yes.

"No you don't, fatty," Anna's voice said.

One brownie has a lot less calories than they would've fed me in the hospital. I'll eat like a pig in treatment tomorrow. I might as well start stretching my stomach now. Not to mention, they look so good.

"You have no self-control. Do you think fitness models eat brownies whenever they want? No, they restrain themselves. Stop being weak."

But tomorrow—

"Tomorrow is a whole day away. You know you shouldn't."

The muscles in my arms ached, my foot bounced, and my jaw shook. Before Anna could make another remark, I grabbed the brownie and took a bite. But the second I started to chew, Anna pressed me with the weight of guilt. Fear built in my chest until my tongue seemed to become numb to the taste of chocolate.

"Stupid. Stupid. Stupid. You aren't good for anything. You will fail at life if you can't stop yourself from being a fatty. It's not that hard. You are weak. You don't need it. You're about to leave your boyfriend for treatment. You don't deserve it."

Anna's voice caused me to drown in a relentless current of regrets, one that I was too weak to fight against. I needed to spit out the bite of brownie. But when I looked up, everyone at the table watched me. If I spit it out, I'd look like even more of a freak than I already was. I had no choice but to swallow.

"Now you've done it. Fine, swallow. But don't you dare eat any more."

I forced the muscles in my throat to do their job. The bite slid down my throat. The simple act of swallowing should be easy, but it wasn't.

I slid the plate back to Jax.

"You don't want it?"

"No, you can have it."

"Are you su—"

"Yes." My voice came out a lot louder than I'd intended. I cringed at the volume. "Sorry, I just . . ." I stood. "I need to go."

I started toward the lunchroom's exit, but soon Jax caught up with me.

"Wait, Ariel. Are you okay?"

I didn't answer.

"Do you still want to go out after school?"

In my desire and subsequent mental fight over the brownie, I'd somehow forgotten about those plans. My brain laser-focused on one thing and left out others. I focused on him. "I'm sorry. Yes, I'd still like to go out with you."

He led me to a corner by an English teacher's room. "Are you okay?"

"I don't want to talk about it."

He rested his hands on my shoulders and looked me

straight in the eyes. "You sure? I can call your mom if you need me to. Do you feel all right?"

I stepped out of his reach, ashamed of the way I reacted to taking a bite of a stupid brownie. What was wrong with me?

"Jax deserves someone better than you," Anna said.

She was right, but I was selfish. I wanted him.

"I'm fine." Before I could say more, Jax filled the distance between us and wrapped me in an embrace. His closeness calmed my frenzied heart and terrified mind. I melted against him, the warmth of his body seeping into mine. I acted crazy, yet he loved me anyway. There wasn't a handbook entitled *How to Treat Your Anorexic Girlfriend*, but Jax seemed to be writing one. Although that handbook would probably come with a fine-print warning: *Complying with every suggestion in this book may still result in the death of your significant other.*

Jax shouldn't have a girlfriend who required a warning label.

"I want to help," he said against my ear.

I pulled back, fighting tears—but I didn't want to cry, so instead I pasted on a smile. "You are. More than you know." The way he and Hope stuck with me spoke more than words ever could. But I was the Titanic and all the lifeboats were taken. I didn't want them to sink with me.

Jax kissed the corner of my mouth. When I relaxed, he kissed me again, this time on the lips. The gesture calmed me even more. "Where are you going?"

"To my locker."

"Want me to come?"

"No, I'll text Hope."

"You sure?"

"Yeah. I'll see you after school."

He pressed his lips against mine one last time, and then he turned to leave. I watched him walk away with a sinking feeling in my gut—a feeling that told me our love story wouldn't last.

I'd never thought of our future before, but in that moment, it looked short.

As if our relationship was taking one of its final breaths.

SCHOOL PARKING LOT

3:00 PM

Jax found me by the back doors. "How was the rest of your day? Do you still want to go out? I could bring you home if that's what you want." But I could read in his expression that he wanted to be with me.

"I'm okay. We can go." The bite of brownie had haunted me throughout the rest of the day. It was torture, not knowing what Mom had planned for dinner. I calculated calories, then calculated them again. The mental toll exhausted me.

Jax smiled. He set a hand to the small of my back and pressed me forward.

My skin warmed at his touch. It was like heat waves that escape from a hot oven as soon as the door is opened. The whole of my back burned, which was nice, considering how cold I'd been all day. "Where did you want to go exactly?"

He pulled me against his waist as we crossed the parking lot. "I was thinking the vintage coffee shop. You know, the one with the weird-hanging lights and stuff."

The way he kept me near him increased the temperature of that oven-hot sensation. More like a melt-your-skin-off kind of hot. He talked about how the coffee shop looked more like an IKEA display room rather than an actual place of business.

He went on and on about the lights of the coffee shop, how they had been re-purposed mason jars. There was even an entire wall dedicated to displaying these jars. They actually had mint growing on the inside of them. The baristas would trim the plants, and then they'd use the herb in teas and seasonal drinks. The place sounded cozy and perfect.

But Anna's voice in my head grew louder and louder as she nagged me, telling me it was a bad idea.

"I know the place you're talking about." I said. "We can go there."

Jax showed off that adorable too-wide smile of his.

We approached his car in the parking lot, and the door screeched as Jax opened it for me. He drove an old Honda CR-V that had two tires in the junkyard, and he filled them with air on his way home from school once a week.

As Jax drove through busy intersections and past neighborhoods, he filled in the silence by sparking conversation about both of our families. Jax preferred to stay off of the highway because of the Honda's unpredictability. He'd had service done on it several times that year and didn't want to push too hard.

My chest tightened as we neared the coffee shop. The lunch spectacle replayed through my mind. What did Jax's friends think of me? I didn't have to worry about calories if I ordered a cup of green tea. Jax and I would talk and have a good time. But anxiety forced me to shove my hands beneath my thighs, and I bit my lip as Jax pulled into a parking space. If I walked inside I'd see the display of muffins, brownies, and breads behind glass. The temptation would pound on one side of my head while Anna pounded on the other. I tried to hide my concern but probably didn't do a great job at masking it.

"Are you okay?"

My eyes burned with tears. Why was this such a big deal? It shouldn't be. I should be able to go on a coffee date with my boyfriend without having a panic attack—but I couldn't. Instead, a hot tear ran down my cheek. "Can we go somewhere else?"

He must have thought of the incident at lunch too. "Want me to take you home?"

A scream built in my chest, threatening to manifest itself. Jax and I had less than two days to spend together. "No. I don't want to go home. Can we just—I don't know. Find somewhere to sit?"

Jax glanced out the window at the coffee shop, then turned back to me. "You sure?"

No. No. No. The words were on the tip of my tongue, but I couldn't say them. Instead, I simply said, "Yes, I'm sure."

Jax's gaze skirted toward the road and then across the parking lot. "I'm not sure where to go."

"Just drive."

With a brief sigh—one that didn't exactly help with my guilt—Jax put the car in gear, then merged back into traffic. We were few miles out when I spotted an abandoned strip mall and said, "Pull in there."

"Why? There's nothing there."

"Please?" I didn't want to go home, and I *really* didn't want to cry in front of Jax. But one of the two was inevitable. And if I were honest with myself, I would have rather cried where only Jax could see rather than start a scene somewhere in public.

Besides, I'd already reached the max of my humiliation tolerance for one day.

Jax did as I asked. He parked behind the empty mall, sliding into a space near a field of overgrown grass—a field with signs of new a development, "Coming Soon."

I reclined my seat, curled my body toward the door, and released the buildup of tears. I couldn't seem to free myself from Anna. She was like a life-sucking leech, and her constant voice in my head had prevented me from having a date with my own boyfriend.

After a moment, Jax's hand rested on my hip. Gentle yet reassuring. "You okay?"

I almost laughed. Of course I wasn't okay. What he meant to ask was, "How can I fix this?"

And in that moment, all I wanted was for someone to hold me the way Mom used to when I was a kid. The times when my feelings were hurt by a friend, or when Dad went on a business trip and neglected to call and tell me that he loved or missed me.

I gestured at Jax, inviting him to move closer to me. The seat shifted as he settled behind me, wrapping his body around mine. I lifted my head, and he moved his arm for me to use as a pillow as I cried harder.

As much as I loved Anna, I hated her even more.

The ugly crying soon gave way to regular crying. I turned to face Jax.

He stared at me, and he didn't seem disgusted by my blotchy cheeks or leaking eyes. "Can I kiss you?"

A small laugh escaped me. "Ew, Why would you want to kiss me now?"

"I want to make you feel better."

"I'm not sure you can."

"What do you need? I want to know how I can help."

I pressed my face against his green shirt. "I don't even know how to help my own self."

Jax rubbed my shoulder, and something in my stomach bubbled like soda fizz. He gave me a look that pleaded with me. I could tell he was desperate to take away my pain, desperate to offer some kind of help.

But the problem was, I didn't know *how* he could help. All I knew was that I needed his comfort.

So I tilted my head and kissed him. His hand cupped the back of my neck as he used his other to continue rubbing my shoulder, as if the act of doing so could erase the pain.

The kiss was different than any of our others. In that moment, I gave him more of my heart—and, somehow, he knew.

Jax stopped rubbing my shoulder, and instead he wrapped his arm around my waist, pulling me against him—so tight that it became hard to breath. I tasted my own tears.

And then I released more tears. Not because my life was breaking, but because someone actually wanted to fix me. I might have been beyond repair, but Jax at least wanted to try. He saw that I was worth the effort. And because of that, I didn't want to stop kissing him and allowing him to hold me.

Anna's voice disappeared from my mind as I let him kiss me harder and longer than ever before. Desperation caused me to grip the front of his shirt. I was frantic to escape my own mind and be with him instead. When I was with Jax, I didn't worry about being ugly. I yearned to remain in that moment.

I knew we were getting carried away, but I didn't care. My heart hurt, and being close to Jax eased the confusion and anguish that I didn't know how to handle.

The bubbles in my brain stopped popping, and soon all I heard was fizz. Jax's hand moved to my leg. His fingers glided up my thigh and then rested on my stomach. He stopped kissing me long enough to look me in the eyes as if asking for permission. "Okay?"

I hesitated at first as panic momentarily burned away my desires. I hated my body. Wouldn't he hate it too?

But I noticed something: Jax didn't look disgusted. In fact, it looked as though he actually wanted me.

He wanted me? The idea was intoxicating. I wanted to be wanted. A lump grew in my throat as I gave a small nod.

Jax touched his lips against my cheek, stopping a tear in its tracks. I closed my eyes. I yearned to feel loved, and Jax offered to give me his love. Why not accept it?

The rest of my world—my issues and never-ending broken-ness—were paused as my thoughts and emotions were consumed with Jax. Our longings collided: My neediness found completion in his desperation to help.

You know how, when you shake a kaleidoscope, the beads shift in all sorts of directions? As a kid, I used to face the tube toward a friend, assuming I'd be able to see them in a more magical light. But then I'd lift the kaleidoscope to my eye and realize I couldn't see my friend at all. The image wasn't what I had expected.

My childish ignorance couldn't make sense of it. I'd stare at the tube in confusion, wondering what could've gone wrong. The beads were lovely, so shouldn't it have made my friend dazzling too?

But it didn't.

The beauty was just an illusion.

Up until that moment in the parking lot with Jax, that's how I imagined it'd be like to sleep with a boy. Like the beads of that kaleidoscope. Beautiful and breathtaking. I thought being with him would make me feel better. As if his love had the power to take away my pain.

Jax didn't do a thing wrong—it was me. *I* was the one who gave him permission.

I'd overheard some of my classmates in school talk about sleeping with their boyfriend of girlfriend. They always made it seem as if this was something to look forward to.

But no one, not one person, spoke of the aftermath. They didn't prepare me for the disappointment that came from giving your all to a boy—only to have the ache inside intensify rather than diminish. Because as we straightened our clothes, that's exactly what I discovered.

The emptiness was even deeper than before.

Along with my wanting to feel better, I also imagined that being with him would make me feel beautiful somehow. But it didn't. How could something that promised to make me beautiful, loved, and cherished leave me hollow inside?

Afterwards, Jax faced me and held me in his arms. But the same hurt that drove me to be with him moments ago still had its grip on me, causing me to hunch forward.

Jax pressed his forehead to mine. "I want to help."

"I know," I whispered.

"Tell me how."

"Just keep being you. Keep loving me." But even as I said the words, I knew something had shifted. There would be no more "us"—at least, not in the same way it had been before. We had too many things between us, especially with me having to leave.

And now this.

That was another thing no one warned me about. How a relationship would no longer be the same after you take it to the next level. *Would it make sense for me to tell Jax I love him? Or should he say it first instead?* These were the questions that bombarded me in the silence of his car.

Jax must have sensed the tension too. He turned on the radio as he drove me home, giving us both a break from struggling to decide what to say.

Because neither of us knew how to fill that awkward silence.

Home

6:00 PM

After crying until my cheeks were hot enough to melt my face off, I wet a washcloth with cold water and draped the entire cloth across my nose and cheeks.

My heart hurt too much to argue about eating dinner. I was still angry with myself for the bite of brownie, and I was also confused by what happened in the car.

Mom made lasagna, garlic bread, and Caesar salad. After only five bites, my stomach cramped—but I didn't care. Something inside of me had broken, and I needed the numb feeling that could come from stuffing myself with food. I'd been through this phase several times in the past. I'd starve myself until I slipped up. Then I'd feel guilty, and eat until I wanted to die.

For once, Dad steered the conversation. "Irma hit Barbuda and St. Martin today. Almost wiped the islands completely off the map."

It took a moment for me to comprehend what he was talking about. The hurricane. With all that had happened, I'd somehow forgotten about its threat.

Dad interrupted the silence. "I'm flying to Boston tomorrow."

Mom took a sip of water, then asked, "How long will you be gone?" The ice in her glass clinked as she set it back onto the place mat.

"Maybe a week. I'm interviewing a possible manager for the new hotel."

Dad frequently traveled for work. After his fifth hotel took off, he bought a bigger house for us, one that was located in a nicer neighborhood. Which is why Jax was no longer my back-yard neighbor.

"Well, the models show that the hurricane is heading toward Florida," Mom said. "We'll be fine. I'll get Ariel settled tomorrow, and then I'll stay with my mom until the storm passes. I'm sure we'll be okay here in Central Florida."

Mom loved Florida. She was born with sand between her toes, as well as a buoyant body. I'd often wondered if she were created to live in water instead of on the actual land. Her skin tanned to the perfect shade, yet it never seemed to burn. She was Florida through and through.

Looking back, I realize I should have been more worried about the storm. But at the time, I was more concerned about being within ten feet of my boyfriend.

Not a hurricane that wasn't exactly guaranteed to hit our state.

Kitchen

9:00 PM

I hated binging, but I couldn't help myself. The rampant emotions of sorrow and worthlessness transformed my appetite into a hungry dragon. The only way I could make the dragon happy? By feeding it. Otherwise, it'd keep nagging me until I ate.

I stood in front of the open freezer, a soup spoon in one hand and half a gallon of chocolate brownie-flavored ice cream in the other.

Goosebumps dotted my legs as I shoveled ice-cream into my mouth. If my life had been a baseball game, then I knew I'd struck out. I ran through the list of disappointments and stabbed the spoon into the carton again.

First, I'd hoped that being a freshman in high school would give me some sort of social standing. When that didn't happen, and my friends from middle school left me, I faced disappointment.

Second, I'd surmised that Anna—and the weight loss— would make me desirable. But, once again, I was met with disappointment. While Anna and I traveled the path toward a lovely existence together, we still had a ways to go. Seven more pounds if I were estimating correctly.

Third, I'd always thought being with a boy would nurture the woman inside. As if, by being in a relationship, I'd magically possess the kind of elegance that women portrayed in romance movies.

That must have been what I was hoping to find with Jax.

In summary, I had no social standing. I strived for a seemingly unattainable kind of beauty. And, on top of that, I found sex to be more physical than soulful.

Rather than licking the ice cream I held in my spoon, I shoved the entire spoonful into my mouth. Who cared what it tasted like? As long as it filled me so full that my gag reflexes could be triggered. My stomach needed to hurt as much as my heart did.

As the cold, sugary cream slid down my throat, I made a decision. That night would be the first time I'd successfully force myself to throw up. I hated to puke when I was sick—but later that night, I would do it on purpose.

Anna tried to reason with me. "Don't you know that you're backsliding in your progress by eating like this?"

I'm going to treatment, anyway. So, what if she was disgusted with me? There was no stopping this train wreck.

Mom and Dad were already fast asleep on the other side of the house. They'd grown accustomed to me staying up late in front of the TV.

Anna didn't have to say a word. Her disapproval, even in the silence, screamed at me.

Well, she could just shove her perfect body into a bottle and throw herself into the ocean for all I cared. Maybe Hurricane Irma would take her out to sea, away from me.

I jabbed the spoon into the container again and shoved another spoonful into my mouth. The insides of my cheeks grew numb. I ate until the half-gallon was gone—as well as all of the feeling in my face.

I threw away the carton, found a very old-looking box of cookies, and tore the seal.

BATHROOM

10:30 PM

Anna told me to stick a toothbrush down my throat to get rid of the food. But if I moved, then I might not need it. My stomach cramped. The millions of calories I'd consumed pressed against every cell of my abdomen, threatening to make a reappearance.

"It's easy," Anna said.

I looked at the pink and white toothbrush that I held between my fingers. I'd tried this before. I opened my mouth and lifted it to the end of my lips. I took a breath and—pulled it back out.

I can't.

"Yes, you can."

Sweat formed on my upper lip, and my forehead grew clammy. Nope, I wouldn't need the toothbrush after all. I tried to relax and let my body release, but the part of me that hated the act of throwing up pressed the bile back down my throat.

Apparently, I couldn't even *be sick* the correct way. I was a failure.

My body didn't expel food; instead, it forced out tears. I was surprised I could produce more after my crying session earlier that afternoon. They were hot and heavy, dripping like syrup from my lashes. Hunching over, I forced myself onto my feet. I slammed the toilet lid down with a crack so loud that I feared I'd wake up Mom.

As I straightened myself, dots formed along the edges of my vision and moved toward the center of my eyes, obscuring my sight. My heartbeat slowed, and I struggled to take in a full breath. My body sagged against the cold white bathtub as I drifted.

When my vision cleared, I lifted my head and squinted at the white bathroom. My chest hurt, and a spike of pain shot up my leg—probably caused by the weird angle I'd settled in. I maneuvered to a more comfortable position and leaned my head against the tub. I could feel my heartbeat pulse throughout my body.

Some people describe hearing their pulse rage in their ears, but I felt mine beat like a steady drum. This wasn't the first time. But with the hospital warning from yesterday, this was the scariest.

I lifted my shirt and observed my bloated stomach. My

body was so thin and stomach so full that the palpitations from my heart kicked my stomach with each beat. It was like there was a baby inside of me. Each pound of my heart caused my stomach to jump. The sensation was both fascinating and frightening.

My body still struggled for air. I forced myself to relax as my mind started a marathon.

I'm dying. This is it. I should've gone to the hospital yesterday.

"This has happened before, Ariel. And you're still here, aren't you?"

It feels different this time. I should get Mom. She can bring me in right now.

"No, just go to sleep. You'll be fine in the morning. You'll be in treatment in less than twenty-four hours anyway."

But what if I don't wake up in the morning?

Anna's words sunk in. I'd be in treatment at this time tomorrow. What did a few hours matter?

When I gathered enough willpower to stand and walk, my legs led me into my bedroom rather than toward Mom.

Anna still wanted me to throw up, but I couldn't do it. I fell asleep with her voice taunting me in my ear. "You'll be okay, Ariel. Someday you'll look in the mirror and love what you see. It won't always be this way. No matter what happens, I will always be here for you."

I wanted many things in that moment, but Anna certainly wasn't one of them. I was sick of the way she made me feel. I was scared, and I hated reliving the way Jax's friends had looked at me in the lunchroom.

It was her fault. All of it.

If it wasn't for Anna, then I wouldn't have freaked out over a small bite of brownie. If it wasn't for her, I would have gone to that coffee shop. I wouldn't have cried into Jax's shoulder. I wouldn't have felt my heartbeat pumping my stomach.

Maybe I could have had a shot at being normal if Anna wasn't in my life.

For the first time since I could remember, I actually *looked forward* to admitting myself to treatment.

Because maybe it could give me an opportunity to kill Anna once and for all.

Chapter 5

Present
   January 31st, 2018

HOPE TURNS the steering wheel of her red Subaru Impreza Hatchback into the gas station parking lot after school. "Want to get something to drink while I fill up?"

I shrug. "Sure. You want anything?"

She parks beside a pump and pops the fuel door open using the lever beside her chair. "Skittles would be perfect. The biggest bag you can get."

I give a nod and step out of the car.

"When are you taking the driving test?" Hope asks, sliding her credit card into the slot.

"Hopefully the end of March or beginning of April. Why? Are you sick of driving me home?"

She pulls the card out and adjusts her hat. "Heck no. I'd love for you to stay license-less. Who's going to buy my snacks after you pass your test?" She types her zip code into the screen and hits enter.

"I still don't have a car."

The machine beeps, and she grabs a nozzle. "Touché. Glad I still get you for a while. Now hurry up. I want my Skittles."

I roll my eyes and say, teasingly, "Maybe if you didn't hold me up then I'd get your candy faster."

She sticks out her tongue at me.

The gas station smells like hot dogs and soda. Before searching for a drink for myself, I find a bag of Skittles for Hope. I'm sure she'd be happy if I ate something. With that in mind, I grab a bag of cheddar popcorn for myself. Popcorn is a low-calorie snack I allow myself. A safe choice.

I reach into the cooler, shuddering from the sudden cool air, and grab a glass bottle of unsweetened iced tea.

I head toward the counter with the snacks in one hand and drink in the other. Rounding the corner of an aisle, I accidentally step into someone's path and jolt back—but somehow, I trip over my feet and lose balance, falling toward a chip display behind me. A hand reaches out and steadies me just in time. But my grip on the bottle loosens and slips from my arms.

Clink.

Before I can check to see if the bottle is broken, the stranger has already reached down to grab it for me.

And that's when I realize that he's no stranger at all.

His eyes meet mine as he hands the bottle back to me—and we both freeze.

"Sorry," I say, taking a step forward to move past him. But I halt when I notice the gas station logo on the lapel of his shirt. "You work here?"

Jax, the boy I've spent almost two weeks writing about, smiles like he's happy to see me. He nods. "When I'm not in class."

I haven't seen him much since the first two months of school before I went to treatment. We mostly saw each other in the lunchroom, but now he attends school in the mornings and takes community college classes in the afternoons. Apparently he works here, too. I faintly remember now.

I take a step back and look down at the snacks I hold. There's no way I can make eye contact with him. "How's college?"

"Like high school, I guess. Except nobody cares if you're on your phone or listening to the lecture."

When my eyes meet his again, I discover that he's still smiling. Why is he talking to me? I'm surprised he hasn't told me what a horrible person I am and asked for me to leave.

I want to move past him, but something keeps me immobile. "How's your mom and brother?"

He reaches behind me and straightens some of the chip bags that I'd bumped into. "Good. Mom still works at the doctor's office, and Lex is still addicted to video games. Nothing new." The bell above the door rings. Jax studies the customer and then looks back at me. "You look ... better."

How should I respond to that? I decide on a simple, "Thanks."

Jax scans the store for the customer. A middle-aged man peruses the beer coolers.

With a sigh, Jax turns back to me and says, "Well, it was nice to see you, Ariel." He turns to go—but I surprise both of us when I grab his arm.

"Jax ..." I release my hold. "Look. I'm sorry for—"

He cuts me off. "Don't worry. It's fine."

Does he realize who he's talking to? "No. I mean, I shouldn't have—"

"We both made mistakes, Ariel. I regret ... "

The cooler door snaps shut.

"Sorry," he says. "I've gotta go."

I watch as Jax hurries to make it to the cash register before the man does.

I make my way toward the counter too—snacks and drink still in hand. I remove a five-dollar bill from my pocket and wait for the man ahead of me to finish paying for his beer and cigarettes.

When it's my turn to check out, I can tell that Jax struggles to make eye contact with me. The scanner beeps as he waves my drink in front of it. I wait for him to say more, but he stays silent.

Almost as if we really were only strangers after all.

It's not until he gives me my change that he offers me a half smile. I lift the corner of my lips in return. I'd love to ask him to finish the sentence he had started. Curiosity skewers me like a toothpick inserted into a pan of brownies, checking to see if they're cooked on the inside.

What does Jax regret?

Me?

Or what happened afterwards?

I give Jax a quick and awkward, "Thank you," before grabbing my purchases and heading outside.

I've always regretted how things ended between us. But what does *he* regret?

The Wednesday after our—well, you know—was worse than a Hawaiian pizza. I regret how ugly my brain was. I couldn't think straight or even act like a decent human.

If only I hadn't allowed myself to fall so far away from who I truly was.

The girl I am now.

The girl without Anna.

What would Jax think if he knew all the battles I've won and lost over the past five months?

Hope is already in the car when I slide in and toss her the Skittles.

She rips the bag open and dumps the candies into her mouth. She starts to turn the key in the ignition, but then she stops and looks at me before putting the car in drive. "Is something wrong? You look like you're in shock."

I finger the bag of popcorn. "Jax works inside."

Her head jerks toward the front door. "Here? Now? Like, are you referring to *this* gas station?"

"No, the one across the street." I give a sarcastic laugh. "Of course I'm referring to this one."

"Did you talk to him?"

"Sort of."

She leans close, as if the proximity will make me tell her everything. "What did he say?"

"That I look better— and that he regrets something."

She removes her key from the ignition and says, "Like what?"

"I don't know. We were interrupted." I point to her keys. "What are you doing?"

She thrusts the car door open. "Gonna find out what he regrets, that's what I'm doing."

"Oh no, you're not." I lean over and pinch her sweater, pulling her back inside. "Leave it be."

"But don't you want to know?"

"Of course I do. But you can't just go in there and demand to find out what he was referring to."

Hope settles back in the car and closes her door. "I can't believe you won't go in there and ask him."

Anger contorts my face. The truth is, I'm afraid to hear what it is that he regrets. "Just leave it, okay?"

She holds her hands up in surrender. "All right, fine. But you know this is gonna nag at you."

The car jerks forward with its shaking transmission as Hope taps the gas. I look at the gas station window. Jax stands directly behind it, staring through the glass.

Watching us as we leave.

Chapter 6

Wednesday, September 6th, 2017

MY BED

6:10 AM

The morning after my binge session, my stomach was in so much pain that it rivaled being legitimately sick. I groaned as I propped myself on my elbows and remembered the night before. A surge of relief filled my chest as I realized I'd woken up at all. *Thank you, God.* Then my chest tightened at the dread of treatment.

Anna's voice found my ears. "You aren't still thinking treatment is a good thing, right? We could still find a way out of this."

My head throbbed. If I could force myself from bed, I could get a few aspirin pills. They didn't have calories, right?

"You could run away."

I rolled my eyes. *No way. I don't have a car, or even a driver's license for that matter.*

"Do you understand what they'll make you do in treatment? Eat, eat, and eat. No exercises. Not even a little."

I know.

"And you're okay with that?"

I'm scared—so, yes.

"You're an idiot."

At least I'm alive.

The moment I tried to get out of bed, my body shook, almost making me believe I had a fever. Peeling the covers off of me was like separating a Fruit Roll-Up from its wrapper.

Unable to part with the warmth and comfort, I pulled the sheet free of the bed, wrapped it around myself, and shuffled into the bathroom.

I turned on the shower and then watched water sputter and shoot out of the showerhead. The only thing that successfully warmed me was a hot shower. This would be the last one in this house for a while.

7:00 AM

Kitchen

I was one hour closer to treatment. I made a pot of coffee and poured it into a travel mug. I didn't exactly have anything against *coffee*, just coffee shops and their accompanying display cases of tempting goodies.

Mom stood at the kitchen counter beside me, her attention plastered onto the weather channel. A giant swirling donut filled the screen.

Hurricane Irma blasted the Caribbean, but forecasters couldn't predict if she would hit Florida yet. And if she did hit Florida, would she travel up the East Coast or hit the Gulf Coast? Images lit the screen of trees that were lashed by gusts of wind and skies that were the color of dark purple frosting. Next, the screen showed images taken from an aerial view—

pictures of torn homes and flooded land—and then it went back to the weatherman. He stood in the studio in front of a life-sized graphic of the state of Florida. Spaghetti lines filled the screen, but none could offer an absolute prediction of Irma's upcoming path.

I screwed a lid on to my travel mug. "Did Dad make it to Boston?"

Mom nodded but couldn't seem to look away from the screen. "He's on his way. I doubt he'll be able to fly back on Monday though."

Her worried expression made my brow furrow. Mom didn't get scared easily. "Should we evacuate?" As if on cue, the TV showed images of cars, bumper to bumper, along the highway. It looked as if the entire population of the state of Florida was evacuating at the same time.

Irma was too big to ignore now. It dwarfed even my admittance to treatment.

Mom finally tore her gaze from the TV and looked at me. "It'll most likely hit the East Coast. We're far enough inland that we should be all right. You'll need to go to treatment. I'm sure it's safe there."

"But what about you?"

"I'll stay with your grandma."

"Are you sure?"

A sad smile preluded her words. "Yes. My priority right now is to get you into treatment. Are you ready?"

I gave a reluctant nod. I'd already started packing after I took my shower. "Yeah. I'll pack more after school."

"I can pack for you. You shouldn't have waited until the last minute." Mom took a sip of her coffee. "I'll pick you up after school. We'll come home and then leave so we can get there by five thirty."

But the images on the screen didn't look so promising. It made me wish that I could just wait it out with Mom rather than be stuck in a pseudo-home, one that would be filled with other sick girls—as well as a staff who probably cared but would never fully understand. What if I was safe, but Mom wasn't?

She'd lived in Florida forever. She would be okay, right?

Mom stepped toward me and gave me a hug. "Have a good day. Here." She pressed a bag into my hand, one that contained carrot sticks and another peanut butter and jelly sandwich. "For lunch."

I wanted to argue. To tell Mom that I'd eaten enough calories for the next week in one sitting last night. But instead, I shoved the food in my backpack. "Thanks."

I waited for Mom to ask me to stay home, but she didn't. She walked me to the door and gave me a wave as I headed toward the bus stop.

In that moment, I knew the storm was more serious than I'd allowed myself to think. If it had consumed Mom's mind so much, then that could only mean one thing. Irma might do more than cause serious damage. She could also very well turn deadly.

7:48 AM

The bus

I sat alone on the uncomfortable bus bench as my thoughts gravitated toward Jax. I'd placed my backpack on the empty spot next to me, indicating that I wanted to be alone. My ear buds plugged my ears. I tried to tune out the conversations happening around me as the bus rattled through subdivisions.

It was obvious that I needed to break up with Jax. I'd realized it on Monday night at the park when he almost called 911. I was also about to be checked into treatment. Jax wanted to support me, of course. But he was a senior and I was a sophomore. Sure, we'd been friends since we first started talking. I didn't know how treatment would turn out. I was supposed to be there three to four months, but what if I needed extra time? I hated, and I mean HATED, the idea of Jax ending up with a girl like his ex, Hadley.

But he didn't need to be chained to me either.

Somehow, it seemed like it'd hurt less if I was the one who did the breaking. And with treatment, I could claim it was for his sake rather than because of my own selfish insecurities.

The more I thought about our relationship, the more determined I became. I needed to end things while I had a chance.

"Why?" Anna asked. She must have been reading my mind.

Because he's going to break up with me eventually, right? Plus, it only makes sense. I'm leaving. We're only in high school. Everyone knows that high school relationships don't last. This would hurt less than if I were to get out of treatment and discover he's with someone else. If I break up with him, then he can't break up with me.

It was self-preservation, pure and simple. I couldn't believe I was even considering it after the way he tried to help yesterday —but if I waited until he broke up with me first, then I'd be even more crushed.

Anna huffed. "Don't come crying to me when this doesn't unfold the way you want."

It's because of you that my entire life isn't going the way I want. If a girl like Hadley isn't enough for Jax, then there's no way that I can be enough for him.

"You could've ditched me a long time ago if you didn't want me. Don't blame me for your issues."

But you are *me.*

I pulled my ear buds out and squeezed my eyes closed. Maybe this was how Dr. Jekyll and Mr. Hyde felt.

The bus jerked to a stop. A handful of students who were half asleep boarded before we started moving again. I pushed the ear buds back in.

"You need to lose seven more pounds. You're right—if you

go to treatment, he won't want you anymore. You'll gain so much weight that you'll become ugly."

That's not why I'm breaking up with him.

"You're doing it because you're afraid."

So?

"So, stop getting mad at me when *you're* the one who is causing your own problems."

I couldn't argue with her there. She was my problem, sure—but she was also *me*.

Jax was one of the best guys I'd ever met. He cared for his family like he was a man and not an eighteen-year-old boy. He cared for me too.

But I didn't know if I could look at him the same way after what had happened between us. And the anticipation that he might break up with me tore my heart as raw and red as a rare steak.

8:10 AM

My locker

The hallways were less crowded than usual. I hurried to retrieve books from my locker and get to class—without running into Jax yet.

The girl who claimed the locker next to mine dropped her bag onto the floor. She cursed as she spun the dial on the metal door. "Sucks we even have to come to school today. Nobody else is here."

She wasn't talking to me, but I still replied. "Huh?"

She jolted as though she hadn't realized she'd spoken aloud. "The hurricane." The dial clicked, and she snapped the lock open. "Everyone's evacuating north."

"I saw that on the news. But we're not in an evacuation zone. They don't know where the hurricane will make landfall."

She shoved her bag into the locker. When it didn't fit, she kicked it. "Some are saying this is one of the biggest hurricanes to hit Florida in decades. Nobody knows what it'll do. I bet they'll cancel class for the rest of the week. If people are already leaving, then there's no point in even having school."

"The hurricane is still days away from Florida,." I said, retrieving my own books from my locker.

The girl dug through her locker—which looked more like a closet to me. She removed a cotton pullover from the mess and held it up. "I have to sit next to the AC vent in Calculus."

"Yeah, I'm always cold."

"Touché." She grabbed a notebook, pen, and a pack of gum, then she slammed her locker and walked away without making any more comments on the hurricane.

I scanned the halls. She was right.

The hallways were unusually empty.

8:26 AM

Spanish class

Hadley approached me in the one class that we shared. Spanish. She had some sort of sick mean girl's radar that sought out vulnerable girls—and being her ex's new girlfriend apparently put me at the top of her hatred list.

She sat by me instead of with her entourage of entitled life-suckers, the girls who cared more about social media than the people around them. I'm sure there was more to them, but I didn't care enough to find out. Hadley waited until Mrs. Ramos turned her back on the class to write conjugating verbs on the board, and then she leaned toward me.

"I heard you're going to treatment."

I kept my face forward, but my neck tingled. I scraped my teeth along my bottom lip and avoided her gaze.

When I didn't answer she tried a different tact. "Jax misses me. He texts me at night because he still isn't over that I broke up with him."

Why was she talking to me? Curiosity caused me to swivel my gaze her way. Jax said *he* broke up with *Hadley*, not the other way around.

"I told him we were done, but he can't seem to move on."

"I don't understand. *He* broke up with *you*, didn't he?"

She scribbled something onto a notepad, acting as if she were taking notes. "Is that what he told you?"

I gripped my pen, feeling her study me like a menu. But I didn't respond.

"What do you think is going to happen when you leave, huh? You don't really think he'll wait, do you?"

She had somehow tapped into my greatest fear besides treatment itself. "Get over yourself," I whispered.

"You know I'm right."

"If he wants you so bad, then why don't you ask him to take you back?" The tone of my own voice surprised me. Jax couldn't still be in love with her, right?

She faced the board again. "I don't want to lead him on."

"You make your relationship sound like a song you didn't like," I said, keeping my voice lowered so the teacher wouldn't hear. "The song is over, so don't ever press play again." Could Hadley be jealous? Maybe she was grasping at rumors, hoping I'd tell her something personal.

"He won't stay with you."

Fear boomeranged inside my skull at the tone of Hadley's voice. Jax wouldn't stay. He was my first boyfriend—and apparently first love never lasts.

"Maybe he won't," I said.

My comment seemed to have caught her off guard.

"But you don't get to be the judge of that," I added. "Jax and I do. We've been friends a long time."

She remained silent throughout the rest of class. She cast

me pointed looks and hid her phone underneath the table, texting her friends who sat in the back row. I wouldn't be surprised if the texts were about me.

I was proud of myself for being brave and telling her off. I could only hope that my resolve would return for my conversation with Jax. The talk I was almost sure would be the end of our relationship.

10:15 AM

Hallway

Hope approached me between classes. She held a sketchbook to her chest, papers sticking out that were filled with graphite and coal drawings. Her straight black hair hung over her shoulders. "Are you nervous?"

I clicked my phone off—ending the text I'd been writing to Jax—and shoved it in my back pocket. My mind felt like it was filled with translucent bubbles. The bodies of students strolling the hallways became a blur. I squeezed my eyes shut, swaying. A hand gripped my arm.

"Ariel, are you okay?" I couldn't remember whose voice that belonged to.

A wave of dizziness weakened my knees. I remained standing—but then the sensation of being flushed down a toilet made my mind swim. It was as if it were spinning and twirling in downward spirals.

When the sensation had passed, I opened my eyes. Hope held my upper arms as I leaned against a locker. Her book and drawings littered the floor.

"What happened?" I asked as she came into focus.

Her brows were drawn together in concern. "Ariel? Can you walk? Here, let me take you to the school nurse."

Anna's voice startled me. "You don't need the nurse. You cried and binged most of the night. You're just tired."

"Come on," Hope said, reaching for my arm. "I'll help you."

Equilibrium restored, I jerked out of her grasp, angry that she'd witnessed my lapse in sanity. Only crazy girls forgot where they were or who they were talking to.

Anna was right. This was my fault. "I'm fine. I don't need the nurse. I'm going to treatment in a few hours anyway." Sure, the near fainting spell scared me, but I was so close to treatment. I didn't want to be admitted to a hospital first. I'd rather go straight to the source.

Hope kept her hands outstretched as if she were prepared to catch me. But I gave her arms a shove, bringing them back to her sides. "I said I'm fine."

"You should see the nurse."

"Bad idea," Anna said.

Hope scooped up her sketchbook and papers. "If you won't go to the office, then let me at least bring you to the cafeteria. You need to eat something."

After all that I ate the night before, I wouldn't need food for a week. Besides, a tray of food would be placed in front of me later that night, and I'd be expected to eat every bite. If I couldn't, then I'd have to drink a meal replacement smoothie instead—and even then, there was a chance I'd be hooked up to a tube overnight. I wanted a few more hours of control.

"I'm okay. I just . . . didn't sleep well."

Hope gave a gentle touch on my arm. She was a touchy-feely kind of friend. Always hugging or consoling.

"Did something happen that you're not telling me about?"

I pressed a palm to my head. "Everything's fine. I'm just tired."

She took a step closer. "Please, Ariel." Determination gripped her words. "Stop pushing me away."

Hope wasn't the jealous type, but desperation shown in her eyes. It was like she was begging me to invite her back into my thoughts. Back into my life.

"Thanks for your concern, though."

I still loved her as a friend, and I wanted her to understand that. But the truth was, friends in middle school didn't always stay close through high school or college. Sometimes I tried to push her away in moments of weakness because I feared she'd grow weary of my issues and leave. Other girls from my past avoided eye contact with me in the hallways, as if the simple act of looking at me embarrassed them. Hope was the only one who drew closer to me when I did nothing but push her away.

Hope glanced above my shoulder and took a step back. "Text me if you need anything."

Before I could answer, she walked away. I spun around to see what caught her attention.

Jax.

10:30 AM

Hallway

Jax gave me a tight hug. "How's your day been?"

I squirmed in his embrace. Hadley's prying still nagged at me. Did she break up with Jax or the other way around?

"I know about you and Hadley," I said.

He eased back and looked at me. "What do you mean?"

"She's the one who ended things between you two."

Shock and confusion registered on Jax's face. He gave me a tug and led me to the end of the hallway, coming to a halt by the janitor's closet.

The halls were clear. The bell had rung sometime while I was talking to Hope.

"First of all—I broke up with her. Secondly, where's this coming from?"

I didn't answer his question. "Why did you break up with her?"

"Why are you asking me this now?"

"I just want to know."

Jax glanced down the hallway, then lifted his gaze back toward me. "We didn't see things the same way. She thought I didn't spend enough time with her, which was true—but I just couldn't seem to offer her enough no matter how hard I tried."

He closed the distance between us and placed his hand on my hip.

As if on instinct, I wiggled away. I couldn't let him feel my bloated middle.

"Ariel, is this because of what happened between us yesterday?" He shoved his hands into his pockets. "I didn't plan to . . . I just wanted to help, and I . . ."

I couldn't look him in the eyes. I didn't want him to have to wait for me while I was in treatment.

"Ariel, what we did yesterday—I don't want that to change our relationship. If we pretended it never happened, would that make you feel better?"

I gave a shrug, staring at the tile floor. What if nothing changed between us and we stayed together forever? Could I risk my heart and future on the small chance we could have real love?

An image of Hadley's perfect swimmer's body filled my mind. Jax had turned her away. What did I have to offer him?

Everyone knew Hadley would get a swimming scholarship. She planned to study marine biology in college with the dream of saving the ocean.

Then there was me. An average girl with no ambition—other than to find something worth living for and a broken girl at that. I had no passion for saving animals, like Hadley. I didn't play sports or lead any committees or groups.

Where did I even fit in to life?

"Ariel?"

I forced myself to look back at Jax. My heart hurt because of how desperately I wanted to stay. The friendship we had developed spaned throughout our childhood, and now into our teen years. But what other choice did I have?

"I don't know what to do."

Jax gave a gentle touch beneath my chin and lifted my face toward his. "Hey, shhh, don't cry. We can work things out. I'm sorry if this is my fault."

No wonder Hadley was jealous of me. Jax had always been the perfect guy. He opened the door for every girl, and not just the ones he liked. He'd never intentionally hurt me, but treatment would separate us.

Leaving him would be the right thing to do.

I wiped the tears from my face and leaned away from his touch. "Sorry," I said, and then I turned around and headed down the hall. If I'd stayed in his presence any longer, there would have been no way I could contain my emotions.

I heard Jax following me. "Ariel, where are you going?"

"Away."

"Wait. Please." He ran to catch up with me until he was by my side. "At least tell me what's bothering you."

I came to a stop and forced myself to look up at him.

"Is this about treatment?"

Goodbye, I thought. I might see him for the rest of the school year, but he'd graduate and move on. Maybe we could be friends again someday.

I started walking again. "Leave me alone."

"Let's talk about—"

"Stop." I whirled around, surprised by my own anger. "Let me be."

The way Jax suddenly froze—and the look of betrayal on his expression—tore my heart into pieces. Even now, as I write this, I can't seem to shake the guilt that pierced me from causing him that kind of pain. It was written all over his face.

But in that moment, it was one thought that gave me the

strength to walk away. *I can't allow myself to be shattered if I'm the one doing the breaking. Right?*

Wrong.

I was so wrong. Because what I know now that I didn't then is this:

You can't become fractured if you're already broken in the first place.

12:00 PM

Girls' bathroom

I leaned against the wall in the handicapped stall during lunch. An announcement that came through the intercom during last period informed us that school would be canceled starting the next day until Monday, at least. Not that it mattered. I knew I'd have to follow my classes remotely for the next few months.

I hid from Jax, Anna, and Hope. I didn't want to see or talk to any of them. Jax had texted me nonstop since I saw him in the hallway.

Jax: *What just happened? Are you okay?*

Jax: *Ariel, please answer.*

Jax: *I want to fix this. I'm sorry if I hurt you. I didn't hurt you, did I? I'm such an idiot.*

Jax: *Can we talk about this? I want to see you before you go.*

Jax: *Meet me in the parking lot after school? If you don't show up, I'd understand. But I hope you do.*

WHAT WOULD it accomplish to meet him after school? My life was a hot mess.

I remember shoving my phone in my pocket and staring at

the white brick walls of the bathroom, wishing the school day would end. The sad truth is, I was ready to sign myself into treatment.

And leave Jax behind to find a new normal without me.

3:15 PM

School parking lot

Jax sat in the driver's seat of his Honda, the door propped open and his feet hanging out the side. "I didn't think you'd come."

I didn't think I would either. But I couldn't seem to stay away. "I'm here."

Jax waved at the seat beside him. "Wanna sit and talk?"

"Out here is fine."

He got out of the car and stood only inches away from me.

He lifted his hand and hovered it above my arm, as if he wanted to touch me, but then he dropped it. "Tell me what's going on. Are you breaking up with me? If this is about yesterday, I'm sorry. If it's about treatment, I want to help."

My bottom lip quivered. "And what does helping me while I'm in treatment look like to you?"

He frowned. "I thought you said I could write letters to you and visit occasionally."

"Why would you want to do that?"

"Because you're my girlfriend." He said it like it was the simplest answer in the world. His hands fidgeted at his sides.

"You want to wait for me?"

"Of course."

I crossed my arms as if to shield myself from the hurt I was about to project. "I don't think we should stay together."

"Why would you say that? We've been friends since . . . forever."

I stepped back when he moved toward me. "This isn't fair to

you, Jax. You shouldn't be with a girl like me. I'm not worth your time. Find someone who can take care of herself and treat you the way you deserve."

"What the heck are you talking about? *You're* the girl I want to be with." He rubbed his creased forehead. "This has to be about yesterday. Are you freaking out about that? I said I was sorry. I wasn't thinking. I—"

"No." I cut him off. "I wasn't thinking either. But if I had gone to the coffee shop with you, then none of that would have happened. *I'm* the problem. You should have the freedom to sit in coffee shops—not in the back of parking lots. It's my fault, and I need to let you live your life." My throat caught on the last sentence.

Jax grasped my shoulders, holding me in place. "You aren't being yourself. Stop acting like I'm going to walk out of your life. I want to be here. I want to help you."

I leaned in, my forehead against his chest, and couldn't keep myself from crying. "I can't help myself, Jax."

He enfolded me in his arms. "That's why you're going to treatment. I'll wait for you."

The prospect of him waiting made me heave with sobs. What if I didn't get better? What if my time in treatment was a waste? Then I'd still be a mess when I returned.

I pushed away from him. "Don't wait for me." I wiped my eyes and stepped back. "I might not be strong enough to get better. Seriously, Jax. You're my best friend too." Tears streamed down my face. "I don't know how long it will take to fix me—or if that's even possible."

Now, as I write this, I know I was much stronger than I was aware. Bravery and boldness pushed against my heart, begging for release, but I didn't know how to give them the freedom to take charge.

It was only Anna's death that could bring me to that place.

When I stood in front of Jax, I was at my lowest, filled to the brim with fear of my future. In retrospect, he did deserve better. But not because I didn't have anything to offer; rather, because I didn't yet know that perceived weakness could actually be strength in disguise.

But I was a sixteen year old who was in emotional angst. So I pushed him away.

Because ignoring my inner courage was easier to do than tapping into it.

"I should go." I turned to leave, but Jax caught my arm again.

"Ariel. Stop."

I tried to pull away. "Let go." Panic pulsed through my heart. I didn't want to break up with him. Ghosting him would have been better than committing emotional homicide. But both of us needed this. "Please."

"It's me, Ariel. You can tell me anything."

"I already did."

"Don't I get a say in if I want to wait or not?"

The irrational part of my brain told me to run, to escape the hurt—and to escape hurting him. But the same part of my brain decided that hurting him was easier to do than allowing *myself* to get hurt.

"No. I'm breaking up with you. So let me go." I hoped he could tell, by the way my voice strained, that I truly didn't want to do this. But I had to.

His hold loosened, but it didn't break. "Ariel—"

"Let me go!"

Jax released me quickly, as if he'd been burned. A group of three girls appeared from between the parked cars and watched.

All I wanted was a clean break from Jax. I didn't want to see or think about him. I knew better than to let our friendship develop into something more. I should have said no when he asked me to date him.

Combining love into healthy girl/guy relationships is like mixing pizza and chocolate cake. They're great to eat separately, but pepperonis are not sprinkles, and frosting should not mix with garlic butter.

"I'll call you later, okay?"

Tears dripped from my chin. "I'm deleting your number from my phone."

He followed, but I didn't turn. "Why are you pushing me away? Let me help you, Ariel."

I spun to face him, causing him to halt. "It was selfish of me to date you. We're not right for each other." I had to practically force the words out of my mouth. Because the truth was, I knew there wasn't anything he did wrong.

Jax's mouth dropped open, and his cheeks splashed with red, like a drop of red food coloring marring white frosting.

I've always liked Jax. But I haven't always liked myself.

5:30 PM

Whole Healing Treatment Facility

Mom fumbled my suitcase from the back of the car, then she rolled it behind her. The little wheels scratched and clicked over pebbles on the parking lot as we made our way toward the entrance. Double doors whooshed open before us. We walked away from the sticky humidity and stepped into the crisp, cool air of the waiting room. Soft music played from a portable speaker on the admissions desk. Sitting next to it, an air diffuser misted a lavender scent that spread throughout the room. But the oil didn't calm me the way it was supposed to.

After Mom and I sat in plush chairs for fifteen minutes, Mom checked her phone. "Maybe I should look for someone."

Slouching lower in my chair, I breathed in the fragrant air. *Breath in, breath out,* I told myself. *Breath in, breath out. Relax. You'll be all right. Coming here is a good thing.* Worry left me as I inhaled and exhaled. I was in treatment. I would be okay. The nurses on staff would make sure my heart didn't stop beating. I'd be uncomfortable for the first few weeks, but my body would soon adjust.

Footsteps padded along the carpeted hallway before Jennifer pushed through a side door into the waiting room. She stiffened at the sight of us. "Hello? What are you doing here?"

If hearts could stop beating without removing life from the body, then that was exactly what mine did. Mom and I shared a wide-eyed glance. "We're on time," Mom said. "You told us to be here by five thirty."

Jennifer checked the clock, then she took a seat across from us. She crossed her legs and rubbed her hands along her black skirt. "No one called you?"

Mom's voice came out strained and irritated. "No."

Jennifer nibbled on her bottom lip before continuing. "I'm sorry. One of us should have called. Unfortunately, we cannot admit Ariel today. We hope to have a bed available by next Monday or Tuesday, but it depends on the hurricane."

Mom lifted her pointed finger at Jennifer. "But you said you had a bed available today."

Jennifer gave a slow nod. "Yes. But travel into and out of Florida has become a bit of a hassle. The girl who is being released today can't get home. Her family and friends live in northern Florida, but they evacuated to Tennessee and can't pick her up."

"Then why did you tell me that Ariel could be admitted today?"

I sat in stunned silence, trying to process the news. I actually *wanted* to be in treatment now, but apparently that was no longer an option.

Jennifer picked at a fold in her blouse. "I'm sorry for the neglect. This has never happened before, but we literally have nowhere for Ariel to sleep. Things will be difficult as it is if we have to rely on generators for preparing meals and to keep the facilities running."

Mom stood. "Can I please speak to you privately?"

Jennifer stood, straightened her skirt, and nodded. "Certainly. Come with me."

Mom followed Jennifer through a glass door that led into the hallway. Their voices were muffled. Mom gave animated hand gestures as she pointed at me and then the opposite direction, further down the hallway.

I caught the word. *"Die."*

Although I couldn't hear what they were discussing, I knew Mom was fighting for my life.

If I couldn't go to treatment, then should Mom take me straight to the hospital?

Images that I saw on the news—of the hurricane sweeping toward Florida—flashed through my mind. I didn't want to be trapped in a bed with a feeding tube. I'd rather be with Mom at Grandma's house with the scent of lemon and chocolate to comfort me.

Mom crossed her arms, still arguing. There wasn't much she could do but voice her displeasure, considering there was literally nowhere for me to sleep. I guess she felt like she had to do something.

Watching Mom's anger caused the little girl inside of me to hurt. Mom loved me enough to fight for me, but I couldn't even help myself enough to get better.

For years, I'd struggled with anorexia, and Mom had no choice but to watch. She couldn't do anything but allow her only child to practically commit a slow suicide. Today was the day she chose to speak, but her voice couldn't change the circumstances. I wanted to tell her that I'd be better and then walk out that hope—but how? I needed help. Whole Healing Treatment was supposed to be that for me.

After a few more moments of heated discussion, Mom

pushed through the doors and headed back toward me. She seized the handle of my suitcase. "Come, Ariel. We'll be back next week."

Jennifer followed my mom into the waiting room, her hands clasped in front of her. "I truly am sorry. I wish we could help. Stay safe during the hurricane."

Neither of us answered as we exited.

Back in the car, Mom clenched the steering wheel and stared straight ahead, unmoving. "Mom?"

She blinked.

"Mom?"

She inhaled from deep in her chest, stretched her neck from side to side, and turned to me. "What?"

I shrunk back. "What now?"

"I should probably bring you to the hospital. Is that okay?" She didn't want to take me against my will.

"I want to stay with you. For the hurricane. I don't want to be away from you."

Tears glistened in her eyes. "I want you to be with me too."

"Is that okay?"

She surveyed me. "Well, how do you feel?"

"The same." Besides nearly fainting, I was fine. I just needed more water . . . and food. But one thing at a time. She didn't know about the fainting.

Mom faced forward again and sat still, probably pondering the situation we'd found ourselves in. Her eyes darted back and forth like she read something. Her mind must've been working hard, weighing the potential risks of not taking me to the hospital against the comfort of us being together during the storm.

Finally, she turned back to me and took my hand, giving it a squeeze as she said, "You'll stay with me."

I squeezed back. "I'm scared." We both knew I was talking about more than just the storm. The literal one, at least.

Mom didn't parrot the fear that I know she felt too. Instead, she gave a heavy sigh and said, "I know."

7:00 PM
   Home
   Mom paced the house, talking on the phone with Grandma while I sat on the couch and watched a movie. I focused more on texting rather than the TV screen.

ME: *I couldn't get into treatment b/c of the hurricane.*
   Hope: *WHAT?!?!*

I EXPLAINED THE SITUATION.

HOPE: *So, you're staying with your mom?*
   Me: *Yep.*
   Hope: *What are you doing tomorrow?*
   Me: *Packing more things and then going to Grandma's.*
   Hope: *Are you free in the afternoon?*
   Me: *Maybe.*
   Hope: *Let me know.*
   Me: *Okay.*

I COVERED myself with a blanket and checked the texts Jax had sent me over the past few hours.

JAX: *Ariel, plz don't walk away from our relationship b/c you're scared. I'm scared, too, but I want to make this work.*

Jax: *Will you answer?*

Jax: *You should let me have a say in this decision too.*

Jax: *I know you are about to go to treatment. I hope everything goes well. Get better. I'll wait for you.*

Jax: *I love you.*

I THUMBED AWAY from the messages. He'd never told me that he loved me before—so why did he decide to say it *after* I broke up with him?

I flipped through pictures of us on my phone, wondering if I'd made a mistake. He loved me. Should I tell him I loved him too?

I clicked on his messages again and hovered my thumbs above the keyboard. But then I dropped my phone on the blanket beside me and turned my attention to the movie.

Thinking about Jax hurt too much. Life didn't make sense the way it had that morning. When I woke up, I'd planned to still have a boyfriend and be in treatment by seven o'clock that night. But instead, I sat on the couch in my own home—not in treatment—and no longer with a boyfriend.

Chapter 7

P*resent*
    February 6th, 2018

KELLY SITS IN HER CHAIR, calm as a yogi, and says, "You're doing great. The writing here is phenomenal. I'm interested in seeing where you take this."

I want to ask her for a written definition of what she considers to be "great."

A life-sucker?

Grief that keeps you up at night?

Because that's all this stupid journal is doing for me. I hated writing about Wednesday. Especially after seeing Jax the other day. I haven't been able to stop thinking about him. I almost asked Hope to pull into the gas station today after school. Writing about him makes me wish to see him again, to say more to him.

But I wasn't the only one who lied. He did too. I lied when I told him I'd delete his number from my phone. He lied when he told me he'd wait for me.

I've been out of treatment almost two months, and the first time I've seen him was at that gas station. He probably has another girlfriend and doesn't want to admit I was right in allowing him to move on without me.

But what more can I say? I've already apologized. My curiosity hangs onto his unfinished sentence.

"I regret..."

What? What does he regret? The question kills me. I'm debating if I should see him again.

I'm not ready to ask Kelly what I should do. Not ready to tell her that I saw him. She'd ask questions that I don't have the answers for. Maybe my interest in him will go away with time. I know it won't, but I'm okay with not being honest with myself a bit longer. Dealing with things too soon can have their own consequences. And I try not to make rash decisions anymore.

The rest of my session with Kelly is uneventful. She wants me to talk about Anna, and all I want to do is leave. I know, very productive.

Part of my problem is my anger toward Kelly. I'm upset with her for so many things, but mostly for buying me the journal. She's started something that I can't seem to stop. Something inside of me needs to keep writing. I feel compelled to continue reliving those moments until I reach Anna's end.

Maybe Kelly's right. Maybe I will find something there.

And that's why I keep writing. I know my next documentation will be a long one, and all the writing has made my fingers cramp. What if I get arthritis? That's what it's called when your hand gets all gnarled and bumpy like a macadamia nut cookie with too many nuts, right? Grandma has that.

Later, I cuddle into bed with my pen and consider how to start writing about Thursday.

Chapter 8

T hursday, September 7th, 2017

8:45 AM
  My bedroom
  Multiple text notifications filled my phone's screen as I checked the time. Groaning, I buried my face into the pillow. Entering treatment yesterday was supposed to save me from the drama of my breakup. Instead, I woke to an uncertain future regarding my health and an ex-boyfriend who rightfully resented my one-sided decision to end things.
  I read the messages that spanned the night.

1:01 AM Jax: *I meant it when I said I loved you. I should've said it sooner. I'm not trying to sound desperate, but I want you to know it's true.*
  2:19 AM Jax: *Can't sleep. Thinking of you.*

3:22 AM Jax: *Still can't sleep. I wish I could call, but I'm sure you don't have your phone anymore.*

3:57 AM Jax: *I'm an idiot. Sorry for all the texts. But you don't understand what you mean to me. You're not just my gf. You're my best friend. We had a rough spot in middle school—heck, who didn't? —but Ariel, you've always been the closest person to me. Remember when we found a stray cat? I forget what you named him. Do you remember how we hid him in a box in the backyard and fed him dog kibble and milk? And the time we "camped out" in my backyard as kids? That's why I love you. You've been there for so many moments of my life. Don't push me out just because you're afraid I'll leave you.*

4:40 AM Jax: *I just looked at all the photos of us on my phone. I like the ones of you smiling the most. Your real smile hasn't been around since you were 13. Is that when this started? Looking at the pics made me happy to know you're in treatment. Ok, I'll leave you alone for now. Get better.*

I HELD my breath as I re-read the last two messages. He pinpointed two of my secrets:

1. That I broke up with him because I was afraid he'd push me away, and

2. That my eating disorder started when I was thirteen.

No one else had connected the dots to figure out when I'd started listening to Anna, but Jax had discovered it simply because of my smile. I saw the difference when I looked at old photos too. The real me was buried beneath the weight of Anna. My eyes were glazed over with lies, although they used to shine with hope and truth.

And how did he know that I'd pushed him away out of fear.

Against my own self-doubt, I texted back.

. . .

ME: *Hey, I couldn't get into treatment b/c of the hurricane. I'm waiting it out with Mom and Grandma.*

I PRESSED SEND BEFORE I could change my mind.

Jax texted me back before I could get out of bed.

JAX: *Will you meet me?*

I SLID my hand beneath the covers and pressed it against my middle. The bones of my hips stuck out like mountains against the valley of my stomach. My fingers brushed over my belly button, up the rolling hills of my ribs, over my shrunken breasts, and then across the ridges of my collarbone.

Peace settled over me at the evidence of Anna. I know it sounds like a sick thing to say, but feeling my bones brought me comfort. Knowing I could control my body gave my mind a disillusioned sense of confidence.

My body kept working, regardless of my negative treatment toward it.

Looking back, I can now see that my body is an amazing thing. A few days after this moment I'd find out that my organs had begun to shut down—but my heart, cells, brain muscles, lungs, and everything else fought hard to keep me alive. Bodies are hard to kill.

Jax's heartfelt messages deserved a response, so I agreed to meet with him.

ME: *When?*

Jax: *Tonight at five? I'll pick you up.*

Me: *I'll probably be at Grandma's*

Jax: *Give me the address.*

I TAPPED IN THE ADDRESS, and then added,

ME: *Why do you wanna meet? I won't change my mind.*
Jax: *Give me one more chance, okay?*
Me: *I guess.*

9:25 AM
The kitchen

After taking a hot shower for my sanity—and dressing in an abundance of layers—I emerged from my bedroom. I found Mom in the same place she was in the day before, behind the kitchen counter and staring at the TV. The cone that was to depict Irma's trajectory looked like swirled yogurt.

The newscaster predicted the category five storm with winds of 175 miles per hour would hit South Florida on Sunday morning. Three more days.

I grabbed the filtered water pitcher out of the fridge. It wasn't until then, when the fridge door shut, that Mom noticed me.

"Good, you're up. We're going to go to your grandma's and figure out a plan for today."

I poured the water into a glass. "I thought we were staying over there?"

"Yes, but I want to talk to her about evacuating. I'm not sure if we should, and I trust her opinion."

This was the first time that Mom had even mentioned the possibility of evacuating. "But what about getting into treatment next Monday?"

Mom took a sip of coffee from a pink floral mug. "There's no denying that we're going to get hit by this hurricane. It'll affect the entire state. I've never seen one this big. I need to ask my mom what to do."

"Do you think she'll leave?" I grabbed a lemon and an orange from the fruit bowl on the counter.

"I don't know."

I sliced the lemon in half and squeezed it into the water, and then I peeled the orange so I could eat it. The juice made my fingers sticky.

Oranges were okay to eat. They were mostly juice. The high sugar content made me hesitate to bring a slice to my mouth—but if Mom didn't see me eat something, then she'd make me some toast or eggs. I'd rather stick with a low-calorie orange instead.

"I thought you said we'd be okay," I said.

Mom still looked at the TV. "This storm is supposed to be one of the biggest on record. We could be out of power for weeks, not to mention the damage caused from falling trees and flying debris."

I ate another orange slice. The fruit exploded juice in my mouth. The taste made me want to eat other flavorful things—like M&M's, peanut butter, and Doritos.

"When do you want to leave?"

"When you're done eating." Sweet, I could get away with eating only an orange. She would probably be too worried about the hurricane to make me eat more.

Throughout this experience of having an eating disorder, and now writing about it, I've come to appreciate the term, "We are our own worst enemies." It's true, isn't it? I rejoiced at not eating, but I was really celebrating in the fact that I was dying.

It all depends on how you look at life—how you twist the kaleidoscope lens.

. . .

10:40 AM

Grandma's house

It was strange to think that the last time I sat at Grandma's house, I'd been worried about treatment. In the span of a few days I'd gone from hating the idea, to accepting it—and then I had it taken away from me.

Mom shifted on the couch beside me and looked at Grandma. "Mom, if we're going to evacuate, then we need to leave now."

Grandma shook her head. "I've lived through dozens of hurricanes that were predicted to be 'the worst,' and yet I'm still here." Yes, my almost eighty-year-old grandma used air quotes. "I hired a local boy to board up the windows tomorrow."

"But Mom—"

"There's no point. Look at the TV. People are flocking out of the state. The gas stations will be dry soon and you won't get a hotel room unless you drive to Michigan."

"That's a little extreme."

Grandma leaned back against the couch cushions. "It's true. And it's only going to get worse. The closer we get to Sunday, the harder it'll be to find gas. What if cars break down on the highway and you get stuck? Do you want to sit out the storm inside your car? Besides, it might take days for you to get far enough north that you'll be out of the storm's path. You could walk faster than that slow-moving traffic."

"Mark could get us a room in one of his hotels."

I suppressed a giggle when Grandma rolled her eyes like a teenager. "I'm staying here."

"Will you at least consider it?"

Grandma pointed at the TV. "These weathermen are not God. The storm could break into a category three before it makes landfall in Florida."

"That's still a dangerous storm," Mom said.

Grandma slapped her knees. "There's more of a chance I'd

die in a car accident during the evacuation than I am of dying
from Irma."

Mom took a controlled breath. "I'm just trying to help."

"If you want to help, then you can take the list off my
counter and go grocery shopping. I need a few things in case we
lose power."

Mom stood. "Fine. Come, Ariel."

I looked between the two women. Grandma gave me a wink
while Mom huffed toward the kitchen to get the list. I
wondered if Mom and I would argue like she argued with
Grandma someday.

11:30 AM

Grocery store

If I'd been at WHT, then I wouldn't have seen the chaos that
Florida had become. The store was completely out of water.
Not only the one we drove to, but according to the gossip in the
aisles, *every store* in the area. Not a gallon or bottle of water
could be found. Floridians had snatched them up faster than
they could be delivered from out of state and restocked.

One woman lamented that she had to buy five gallons of
unsweetened tea and a few two liters of soda to hold her family
over if the power went out. If someone couldn't buy water, then
they could fill gallon containers from the tap before the power
went out. Why stress?

Mom filled the cart with items from Grandma's list and
anything she thought we might want. Floridians liked to be
over-prepared for hurricanes when it came to food, water, and
batteries—sometimes to the point of ridiculousness.

We maneuvered the cart through the store as gracefully as
bumper cars. Clearly not as many people were evacuating as
Mom thought.

"We might be eating peanut butter and jelly for a few days,"

Mom said as she placed two jars of the creamy kind of peanut butter in the cart.

We made it to the bread aisle and found only tortillas, pita bread, and sandwich rounds—which looked more like flattened hamburger buns. Mom threw one of each of the sad-looking items into the cart.

"Looks like we're having peanut butter and jelly *pitas* instead. We'll bring over the food we stocked up on over Labor Day weekend tomorrow too. We'll get whatever my mom has on her list."

As we continued to shop, the emptiness of the store surprised me. Even the lunchmeat department was almost depleted. Floridians were in full freak-out mode. You'd think more would be wise like Grandma—but according to the preparedness of the natives, the world was about to end. Or at least in Florida. *Who needs ten loaves of bread, fifty gallons of water, or buckets of batteries? Save some for the rest of us.*

By the time we left the store we had a cart filled with random food. I got lucky in the produce section and stocked up on apples, bananas, and carrot sticks. Apparently, when the world was coming to an end, most people didn't care if the food they bought was healthy or not.

12:00 PM

Grandma's house

After waiting in the grocery store line for what seemed like hours, Mom and I finally loaded the car and drove back to Grandma's house. I checked my phone every few minutes to see if Jax had texted me, but he didn't. Maybe he'd cancel. I both desired and hated the idea of us talking to each other.

Grandma was dozing on the couch when we came through the garage door.

Mom plopped a bag onto the kitchen counter harder than

necessary. "Sure, Mom," she said, throwing her voice toward Grandma. "You take a nap while we run your errands for you."

Grandma squinted. "Sounds good, sweetie."

I settled in the recliner and checked my phone.

No new messages from Jax, but one new text from Hope.

HOPE: *Can you get away for a bit? I want you to meet someone.*

I GRIMACED. With all of Jax's texts I'd forgotten about Hope. Who did she want me to meet?

ME: *Can it wait until after the storm?*

SHE RESPONDED FASTER than I thought she would.

HOPE: *No. You need this.*

Me: *Who do you want me to meet?*

Hope: *Her name is Tara*

Me: *Why should I meet her?*

Hope: *I'll tell you when I pick you up. Where are you? I can come now if you're available.*

SHE KNEW WHERE GRANDMA LIVED, and I wouldn't put it past her to come over without an invitation.

I sighed and turned toward Mom. "Can I go out with Hope?"

"Where?"

I shrugged. "I don't know. She wants to introduce me to

someone." An easy way out would be to tell Hope that Mom refused. There was no way she'd let me go, especially when I should have been in treatment or in the hospital.

Mom tossed a packet of pitas onto the counter. "Sure, I'll make you a sandwich first."

"What?"

She unscrewed the jar of peanut butter. "I trust Hope. She's been a great friend."

"But I don't know—" My phone stared to ring. "Hello?"

"Can I pick you up now?"

This was happening way to fast. Anxiety tempted me to take a run for it. "Who do you want me to meet?"

"A friend named Tara."

"Why can't this wait?"

"I'll tell you when I pick you up. Is now okay?"

Mom listened, but she didn't comment on my end of the conversation.

"Fine." I told her where I was. Mom had a pita with peanut butter and jelly on one of Grandma's china plates when I tapped off my phone. The urge to sleep weighed my body toward fatigue. I had to summon the energy to see Hope and meet her friend, as well as to talk to Jax.

The prospect of being held hostage in treatment and shoved full of calories sounded better than being free. My freedom felt out of my control.

12:30 PM

Hope's car

I slammed the door and buckled my seat belt.

"Watch it. No need to get all fussy with my car, now. She has enough problems as it is."

"Who are we meeting? I'm seeing Jax later. I can't stay out long."

Hope chanced a quick look at me as she pulled away from the curb in front of Grandma's house. I squeezed my eyes shut at her silence. I shouldn't have mentioned Jax. Of course she would have heard the rumors by now.

"Ask the question that's on your mind," I said.

She brushed a crumb off her dashboard. "Are you still together?"

I looked out the window, fidgeting with the seat belt. "No."

"Okay."

I jerked my head back toward her. "You're not going to ask me a million questions?"

"Obviously you didn't plan on telling me in the first place."

My shoulders drooped. "Sorry. I didn't mean it like that. It's just . . . there's been a lot going on with treatment and the hurricane. I haven't had time to process everything."

"Will you tell me why?"

I leaned my head against the headrest. "I can't explain it. Let's not talk about it now. Can you tell me where we're going and who I'm meeting?"

Hope pressed the brake and turned the wheel left. "Promise not to get mad at me?" I held my breath, waiting for her to continue. "There's this girl. Tara. She's the wife of the youth pastor at church—and, well, she's struggled with an eating disorder. She's already agreed to meet you."

I clenched the door handle. "Why would you do that? I don't want to talk to anyone. I'm going to treatment. I've met girls with eating disorders before. It's not new."

Hope held a hand up but kept her other one placed on the steering wheel. "Calm down and listen. She only wanted to meet with you if you asked. I may have lied a little and told her that you wanted to see her. I did it for your own sake. Please talk to her for me?" Her voice went up a notch as she pleaded with me.

Watching Hope as she drove, a memory resurfaced—one

from years ago, when we were in middle school. Both of us were laying across beach towels, the Gulf of Mexico behind us as we drank from glass bottles of soda. The sun shone bright and hot. Our toes, poked over the edge of our towels, were covered in sticky sand. Dune grass blew in front of us, and both of us smelled like sunscreen. We laughed as we talked about the boys we had crushes on and the most recent thing our mothers had done to anger us.

The memory faded—but as I looked at the Hope, I could still see the girl she used to be. My best friend.

The same way that my mom had argued with Jennifer at treatment, fighting for my life, Hope was fighting for me too. If I could have changed for the both of them, then I would have. But it was too hard for me to accomplish on my own. Starting recovery and following through with it were two mountainous endeavors.

Since I couldn't change all of me, then I decided to at least give Hope the one thing I could offer in the moment.

"Fine," I said. "I'll meet her."

1:00 PM

Tara's kitchen

Hope and I sat at a salt-and-pepper-colored granite counter top. Modern bare bulb light fixtures reached down from the ceiling, and their reflected light shown in our coffee and green tea. Tara, an African American woman who had her crimped hair pulled back into a thick ponytail at the base of her neck, stood opposite us in front of the kitchen sink. I couldn't tear my attention from her face. A long scar ran down her cheek.

She pressed the lid of her single-cup coffee maker over a fresh pod and pressed the brew button. We watched the machine whir to life and spit mint-scented coffee into her mug.

When the machine quieted its sputtering, she turned to us with her drink.

"I was hesitant to agree to meet with you," she said. "I don't want to intrude on your life, but Hope was insistent."

I ran my finger along the handle of my teacup. "She can be that way."

Tara lifted her mug and inhaled the steam. She looked at Hope. "I'm not sure what you want me to say."

Hope looked between us. "Tell her how you got your scar."

That captured my attention. I set my elbows on the counter and leaned in.

Tara set her mug down and straightened her white T-shirt. "Yes. That." She traced the scar on her face with a finger. "That's actually a long story . . ."

I checked the time on my phone. "I've got time. Does this have to do with . . . ?" I fumbled for the right words. "Hope said you had an . . . ."

When Tara's eyes lifted to mine, she looked at me in a way that no one else had—not my mom, Hope, Jax, a counselor, nutritionist, or any other eating disorder patient.

Tara saw me. She more than saw me—she understood. Just one look at her confirmed this for me. I instinctively knew that I could trust her.

"Eating disorder," Tara finished for me.

"Y-yes," I said. "Hope said you've had one."

"I did, and yes—my scar is part of that."

"What happened?"

Hope must have sensed our bond, because she stayed silent. White kitchen cabinets framed Tara as she stood before us. "Prepare yourself for the saga." She smiled.

"Okay."

She set her mug on the counter. "When I was five, my parents died in a car accident. I was placed in the custody of my aunt and uncle." She fingered the rim of her mug. "I know—

rough start." The way she spoke, the soft tone of her voice, put me at ease. "My aunt worked long shifts at a hospital and didn't have kids of her own. I spent a lot of time at home with my uncle. The first two years of living with them was fine." She paused before continuing. "But when I was seven, my uncle started molesting me while my aunt was at work."

I glanced at Hope. She raised her brows, as if to say, *yeah I've heard this story before, now listen close.*

Tara continued. "By age ten, he sexually assaulted me on a regular basis. My aunt asked me why I never had friends over. I told her I didn't have any close friends instead of telling her the truth. It was partly true. When the abuse became a normal part of my life, I started pushing most of my friends away. I didn't want anyone to know what my uncle did to me. He convinced me that I'd get into trouble if anyone knew, and he threatened to kick me out of his house if I told anyone—especially my aunt. Since I didn't have family other than them, I stayed quiet. I couldn't afford to lose my home. My aunt was a great mother to me, so I figured I should be happy.

"In middle school, I started to save the money my aunt gave me for lunches instead of eating. I thought if I saved enough money then I could run away." Tara gave me a rueful smile. "I had no idea what I was doing. After a few months of not eating lunch, my classmates started to tell me I looked good. I'd never been overweight, but I liked the compliments. I started to equate not eating with control. I could control the money I saved, and the way others thought of me, by controlling what I did and didn't eat.

"By the time I entered high school I was stick thin. When a boy asked me on a date, I was so happy I didn't sleep for almost a week. I couldn't believe someone wanted to spend time with me. My uncle still abused me, but I pushed that to the back of my mind and focused all my energy on my new boyfriend. When my uncle found out I was seeing someone, he went into a rage

and beat me. When she got home, my aunt found me uncon-
scious and took me to the hospital. It was during my examina-
tion when the doctors discovered evidence of sexual abuse."

I sat, trying to mask my surprise. Most people didn't talk
like this, but Tara was different.

"My uncle was arrested for assault and battery. My aunt
insisted that I tell the doctors and police the truth, and she was
heartbroken when I told them all that happened. I could stay in
her custody if she worked fewer hours and spent more time
with me. I was a junior in high school at this point." Tara
stopped. "You good so far?"

I nodded.

"When I realized that I didn't need to run away, I started
buying lunches again—but I couldn't eat them. I craved the
control I felt when I didn't eat. I felt stronger. So I started hiding
food from my aunt and continued to lose weight. She grew
worried and brought me to my doctor. That's when I was diagnosed with an eating disorder. I had starting seeing a counselor
since my uncle was put in jail, but I had to switch therapists to
see one who was specialized in eating disorders."

I sipped from my cup to appear less emotionally impacted
than I was. I could relate to the sense of control and the feeling
of strength that arose from skipping meals. Not eating gave me
a high.

I set my cup back on the counter when she continued.

"In the middle of this, my boyfriend decided to break up
with me. He didn't know everything, so I couldn't blame him. I
was a mess. I graduated high school at a lower weight than
when I'd entered as a freshman. My aunt and counselor
couldn't help me. At college, I lived in the dorms and met
Kenny on my first day."

"Your husband?" I asked.

Tara pointed behind me. "Yes."

I twisted in my chair and saw what she pointed to. A wedding photo. Tara stood in a white dress beside Kenny underneath an awning of white lilies. "He asked me on a date, but I said no. I guess God wanted us to be friends, though, because I found him in my dorm later that day. I almost called the police until I realized he was just as surprised to see me. His older sister, Miriam, was my roommate. I wouldn't go on a date with him, but he still hung around. He and Miriam have always been close.

"I still controlled everything I ate and convinced myself I didn't have a problem. But one weekend, when I was on a drive home to visit my aunt, I passed out and got in a wreck. My car flipped several times, and all the windows broke. A shard of glass punctured my cheek and had to be removed in surgery." She ran her finger along the white scar. "And that's how I got this."

"From the accident?"

"Yes."

"Why did you faint?" I suspected I already knew the answer. And I was right.

"Starvation and dehydration caused me to faint."

Hope and I shared a glance. I knew we both thought about my almost fainting in the hallway. "What happened after the accident? Did you go to treatment?"

"I found a counselor and was able to work toward healing that way, but it was Kenny's sister, Miriam, who inspired me to get better."

My tea was lukewarm, but I drank it anyway. Hope tipped her mug up and emptied it into her mouth. Tara took it when she was done and set it in the sink.

"What did she say?"

"She read song lyrics to me."

I couldn't help but laugh. "You got better because of *song lyrics*?" I listened to tons of music, but none of it moved me toward healing.

"These lyrics are from an old song." Tara closed her eyes and quoted.

"'For you created my inmost being;
you knit me together in my mother's womb.
I praise you because I am fearfully and wonderfully made;
your works are wonderful.
I know that full well.
My frame was not hidden from you
when I was made in the secret place,
when I was woven together in the depths of the earth.
Your eyes saw my unformed body;
all the days ordained for me where written in your book
before one of them came to be.
How precious are your thoughts, God!
How vast the sum of them!
Were I to count them,
they would outnumber the grains of sand—
when I am awake, I am still with you .'"

She opened her eyes.

"That's a song?"

"It's a song from the Bible. Psalm 139:13-20. Miriam read it to me when I was in the hospital recovering from the car accident, and then surgery. When she quoted the Psalm, I envisioned my ultrasound pictures and how much my mom and dad had loved me before they passed. I didn't realize she had quoted the Bible until she told me."

I felt Hope's gaze on me but I kept my attention on Tara.

"The idea of there being a God who cared about me that much both confused and inspired me at the same time. I didn't understand why he'd allow my uncle to hurt me if He loved me so much—but when Kenny and I started to date shortly after my accident, he told me that God was more hurt than I was about my childhood abuse. I still don't truly understand, and some days I'm still angry. But when I focused on the part of God that loved me and knew me before I was even born, that's when I started to feel free."

If Tara didn't understand me on a physical level I may have dismissed her idea of God—but the way she saw me, and the way peace radiated from her drew my attention closer.

"And that's it?" I asked. "That's how you got better?"

She nodded a little. "It was the start. I still see a counselor."

"But you're recovered?" She genuinely believed God loved and cared for her even after she was sexually abused for years. She believed God had created her the same way I liked to create elaborate dinners. Tara believed she was a design of God. But if she believed that God designed her, then why did God design me to be ugly? Why couldn't He just make us all beautiful?

She finished her coffee, rinsed her and Hope's mugs, and set them in the dishwasher. "I'm hesitant to say I'm recovered, but I think I'm close."

I still held my cup between my hands. "What do you consider to be recovered?" She didn't look like she had an eating disorder.

She squinted at an aloe plant by the sink and considered my question. "I think full recovery is when you don't worry about food at all. I think it's a place of freedom from the mind-sets that bind you to your disorder. It's the act of being in tune with your body so well that you can sense what it needs and wants. It took a long time for me to listen to my body, but I've been doing better. There are still some habits I'm working to break."

I wanted to ask what they were, but something in the atmosphere shifted. Neither Hope nor Tara changed their open posture, but I retreated within myself. I loved that Tara was doing well, I truly did—but I didn't know what that looked like for me. I was beyond the point of being able to see a counselor and get better. Both my body and mind needed physical intervention. I could no longer make healthy decisions for myself.

"Does that help?" Tara asked.

Yes and no. Hearing her story gave me a centimeter of hope for myself, but weren't all journeys different? I wasn't entirely sure if I was too late to start mine. "Yes," I said in an effort to avoid more questions.

She must have sensed the shift in my willingness to be open, so she changed the subject. "Where are you staying for the hurricane? The church is a shelter, so Kenny and I will stay there. You, too—right, Hope?"

Hope nodded. "Yep. I'm making my bed in the baptismal."

I burst into laughter. "What? Why? Can you do that?"

She stood. "Sure. Throw a few pillows in there and it's like a bed. I'll pack it with blankets too. It'll be the safest place in the building."

Tara laughed too. "Oh, Hope. No wonder you and Kenny get along so well."

Hope shrugged and looked at me. "I come here for movie night sometimes. Kenny and I like the same movies. *Transformers, Star Wars, Jurassic Park*—you know, the good ones."

"Those sound like teenage boy movies," I said.

She waved me off. "You're no fun."

We talked a little while longer, and then I checked my phone again. Two hours had passed, and I had a new text from Jax.

JAX: *Can I come over sooner?*

"HOPE?"

She read the look on my face. "I guess it's time to go."

Tara gave us each a hug. "You can call me anytime, Ariel, okay?"

"All right." But I wasn't sure I would. I didn't know if I could reach the same health that Tara had. I still had a long way to go. Especially when Anna told me I had seven pounds to lose before I could become beautiful. To be like Tara, I'd have to go the *opposite* direction. No, I didn't want to die—but I also had no desire to gain weight, either.

We left the cute one-story house, which was located in a modest subdivision, and headed back toward Grandma's.

3:00 PM

Grandma's house

Mom accosted me the moment I shut the front door behind me. "Who did you meet?"

I plopped on the chair in the living room. "A woman named Tara."

Mom and Grandma sat on the couch, watching the Weather Channel again. Pages of crosswords and Sudoku littered the coffee table, along with pencils and differing remotes. Mom's raised brow suggested she wanted more information.

"Tara's in recovery for an eating disorder."

She muted the TV. "Oh? What kind?" Mom had become a near expert on the book knowledge regarding eating disorders. She'd read online articles on new classifications of disorders such as orthorexia, drunkorexia, and EDNOS.

"Anorexia."

Mom tried not to overdo her enthusiasm. "How long has she been in recovery? What did she say? How's her health now? Did talking to her help? How does Hope know her?"

I sank into the worn fabric of the recliner and sighed. "Mom . . ."

"Sorry, I'm just curious."

Grandma didn't argue in my defense. They both waited for an answer.

I rubbed my palms along the arms of the chair. "I liked meeting her. She told us her story and said I could call her anytime. She still sees a counselor."

"Who?" Mom also researched eating disorder counselors, but she hadn't been able to get me to see one. At the time she had researched Kelly and her involvement with WHT. She'd told me about her, but I wasn't ready to see anyone. I knew I'd be required to talk to someone soon.

"I don't know, Mom. I didn't ask."

"Can you call and find out?"

"Mom. Stop." I reeled in my frustration. "I *want* to go to treatment."

Her eyes widened. I hadn't yet told her about my change of heart.

"I'll go next week," I said. "I don't want to talk about this with you."

She didn't understand. Book knowledge couldn't explain the fierce war that went on inside my head. The push and pull of love and hate for myself, or the fear that I might lose a battle with my own mind.

"What are the forecasters saying?" I pointed at the TV screen, desperate to change the subject.

Mom opened her mouth, but she must have caught herself before she could ask another question or berate me further. She unmuted the TV with one of the many remotes. "The hurricane is predicted to arrive in Florida Sunday. It could still change course, but it's big enough to affect the whole state. Nobody will be outside of its path. Your grandma and I have decided that you and I will spend one more night at home, then we'll come here tomorrow and stay for the duration of the hurricane."

"When do you think it'll be over?" Mom probably knew what I was *really* asking, which was, *when will I go to treatment?*

She grimaced. "I don't know."

A soft knock interrupted us. I checked my phone and almost cried out when I saw a text from Jax that had come through fifteen minutes ago.

JAX: *Coming over now.*

I STOOD. "IT'S JAX."

Grandma straightened. "Invite him in."

"We're going to talk outside."

Mom and Grandma's heads swiveled to watch me like two curious owls. I waved them off. "I'll be right back."

Jax stood on the welcome mat, his hands shoved in his pockets, when I opened the door. Mom and Grandma still watched, so I stepped out and pulled the door shut. Jax wore a pair of cargo shorts and a white T-shirt. His hair stuck up at odd angles, while his customary smile hid under lips pinched in a tense line.

"Hey," he said.

I imagined Mom and Grandma tiptoeing toward the door and listening like eavesdropping middle schoolers. "Wanna go for a walk?"

"Sure."

We ambled along to the sidewalk and took a left. Grandma lived in an older cul-de-sac. Some houses were well cared for and had trim lawns, flowering gardens, and freshly painted doors—but others had scraggly lawns, overgrown bushes, and neglected exteriors. A brown squirrel rushed across the street and ran up a tree. We passed a home where men had fastened metal hurricane shutters to the windows. They now worked on another house down the street, shiny metal shutters splayed across the yard.

"Thanks for meeting me. I wasn't sure you'd agree to it."

I didn't answer. Walking with him hurt as much as I thought it would. I wanted to hold his hand, hug him, and let him kiss me.

"Jax doesn't really like you. You don't deserve a guy like him," Anna said. She'd been quiet for a while. Sometimes I didn't need to hear her voice to follow her advice. The patterns she'd taught me had become as natural as breathing or sleeping.

But she was right. I didn't deserve a guy like Jax.

Out of nowhere, a different voice countered Anna's. A voice of peace inside of me that was getting tired of her negativity. "Why *don't* you deserve a guy like Jax?"

Because I'm sick, and part of me actually wants to be sick. I'm not the girl he used to know. I'm a broken piece of her. I thought of my kaleidoscope collection and how it took many broken pieces to make one beautiful picture. But my life didn't make a beautiful image. My life looked more like a toddler who mixed every color of paint to create brown. There was nothing beautiful about my brokenness.

"I'm sorry to hear about treatment. I know you weren't looking forward to it, but . . . I was glad you were—I mean . . ."

"I'm sorry too," I said.

His tense shoulders relaxed. "Listen, about yesterday. Do you still want to break up? If I did something to mess things up, just tell me." He kept his hands in his pockets.

Hammers banged as the men behind us fastened shutters to windows. Sprinklers in the yard ahead hissed as they spurted water.

"It's not you," I said.

He removed a hand from his pocket and clasped my arm in a firm-but-caring grip. "Don't give me that excuse. I know you're not at your best, but,"—he pointed at himself —"I've been around for all of it. You aren't scaring me away."

I think, as girls, we all want to be loved. I know I did. But when Jax's love reached a point of such sincerity that it couldn't be denied, I started to get scared. What was the next step in a love like that?

I didn't like the idea of recreational dating. If we reached a place of deep relationship, then we'd start promising forever to each other—and I didn't know what forever looked like for me. Would Anna be with me forever? Would allowing Jax to be with me equate to offering him a box seat to watch my own downfall? I hated watching my mom suffer because of my illness, and I didn't want Jax to suffer too. I'd rather remove myself from both of them and remain in isolation.

"I appreciate you sticking with me, but I think it's time I did this on my own."

"What is that supposed to mean? You can't do life alone. Nobody can."

I didn't plan to face life alone. I planned to fight Anna alone —or succumb to her. "It means, I don't want to be in a relationship. I want to stay broken up," I lied. I didn't want to be away from him, but I saw no other option.

He searched my face as a car idled past. Kids screamed in laughter down the street. He must have found the resolve in my eyes, because without warning he leaned in and kissed me.

His kiss said more than words could, and I almost relented as he set his hand against the small of my back and pulled me closer until our bodies crushed together. For a moment, I lost myself in the kiss. His lips were soft and warm, but soon they tasted like salt.

I was crying.

Jax's breath matched mine as he pulled away and searched my face. With his thumb, he wiped the tears away from my cheeks. His hands stayed warm on my face even after the droplets were gone. He didn't want to let go.

I took one step back, out of his reach.

"What about after you get out of treatment?" he said. "Think you'll feel differently then?" He grasped for something to hold on to, hope that we might be together—but I couldn't predict the future.

"I don't know."

Something in his demeanor hardened. When Jax saw he couldn't change my mind, it was as if he looked for an escape route so I wouldn't see his hurt.

He turned back toward Grandma's house and his car. "You have my number. I'll be waiting." He took a few steps away from me.

"Wait, Jax—don't."

He pivoted back. "Don't what?"

I hesitated first, then responded, "Don't wait."

Crestfallen, he nodded once, and walked back to his car. I stayed where he'd left me, a block away, and watched as he drove off.

I didn't love myself enough to love Jax. Now, as I write this months later, I wonder what he wanted to say to me at the gas station. What does he regret? He did everything he could to stay, but I still pushed him away. There's no way he could still be waiting for me.

Right?

Chapter 9

Present
February 14th, 2018

RATHER THAN GOING on a date for Valentine's Day, I'm practicing driving. Mom has scheduled my test for Saturday, March 17th—and I'm not as confident as I'd like to be. My biggest driving struggle is taking left turns at intersections. I like the lights that have green arrows to tell you when to turn—but solid green lights, or even the blinking yellows, make me nervous.

On top of driving, I can't stop myself from thinking about Jax. If we were together then this would be our second Valentine's Day as a couple.

Mom is in the passenger seat and has one hand gripping the interior door handle while the other clutches her thigh. She's not the greatest teacher. "Why don't you ask Dad to help me? He's in town, right?" Like Anna and myself, Mom and Dad split after the hurricane, but he has an apartment nearby for when he's in town. In a way, Irma also killed my parent's marriage. Well technically, Dad's the one who killed it, but Irma certainly exposed the ugly secrets.

"He's out of town." Mom points at the intersection ahead. "Turn up here."

"Left?"

"Yes. You need to practice."

I try to relax my muscles as I approach the light. Why can't all traffic lights have a left turn arrow? Florida drivers are crazy as it is, so why give them the option to turn left with oncoming traffic? They should let the carefully-constructed light system decide when cars should stop and when they should go.

I click on my turn signal and follow the curve of the lane into the left-turning lane. Of course, the light is solid green and another car follows me on my bumper.

Great. Now I have the added pressure of an impatient driver behind me.

Waves of cars pass at varying speeds. I spot a gap in traffic in the distance. Mom points. "You can go there."

"I see it."

We wait. Since Mom doesn't let me listen to the radio yet, the other sounds—such as the clicking of the turn signal and the whoosh of cars that whizz by—are intensified.

When the gap in traffic arrives, I press the accelerator too hard and dart through the intersection.

I release a sigh of relief, and a satisfied and cocky smile lifts my lips. "I did it."

Mom no longer keeps a life-or-death grip on the door handle. "Start toward home. You've done good today. At this rate, you should be ready by April."

That's the goal. Of course, I enjoy being chauffeured by Hope, but I can't expect her to drive me around forever. I'm seventeen now. I should have a driver's license. Getting my license right after my sixteenth birthday is yet another thing

Anna stole from me. I should take that into consideration as I continue to write in my journal.

There are several ways to get home, but I choose the route that brings me past the gas station, the one where I last saw Jax. The sudden urge to see him makes my fingers twitch on the steering wheel.

Does he have a girlfriend to lavish gifts on this Valentine's Day? His relationship status shouldn't matter to me anymore, but for some reason it does. I want to know what he thinks of me. I don't expect him to love or even care for me after the way I ended things—but it'd at least be nice to know if he's moved on.

I mentally slap myself. Who am I kidding? If I found out that he had a girlfriend, my insides would be torn apart.

As we approach the gas station, I can't seem to stop myself. "Mind if I stop for a snack?"

Mom is silent in what I imagine to be momentary shock. I've been out of treatment several months, and I've asked for a snack maybe a total of six times.

"Sure," she says. "Stop at the Publix by the house."

"Actually, I was thinking we could stop at the gas station up here."

I keep my focus on the road, but I can imagine Mom's face contorting in a mixture of confusion and happiness. Her prodigal daughter is asking for food. It's a miracle. I've been healthy since leaving WHT, but Mom can tell that I still struggle. I'm not what anyone would consider to be a normal high school junior as far as food is concerned—but at least I don't go on crash diets, starve, or binge on pizza or cake anymore. I follow my meal plan and don't deviate from Hanna's written instructions.

"We don't need gas," Mom says, "but okay."

I park at the side of the building rather than the front. I don't want Jax to see me coming inside.

I leave the car engine running and tell Mom, "Be right back." I grab my purse, which contains meager babysitting money, and head for the front.

I am only three steps away from the car and I already want to turn around—but I press onward. I have no idea what I'll say to Jax when I see him, but hopefully the conversation will flow naturally. I'll ask him how he's been, and he'll tell me what he regrets, then I'll find out that he has a date later tonight. Then I'll buy a king-sized Snickers bar, leave, and eat the whole thing alone tonight—and hate myself for it later on.

A college-aged guy holds the door open for me and ogles my backside as I walk in. I don't say thanks because I don't want him to get the wrong idea. I don't have much of a backside to look at anyway and holding the door open for a girl should be standard procedure.

A few people wander the aisles, and customers come in and out to pay for their gas. It's not as busy as more popular gas stations. I scan the store for Jax, but the guy behind the counter —who is surrounded by Valentine's Day candy, heart-shaped sugar cookies with pink frosting, and a few Valentine's Day mini stuffed animals—is not Jax. Instead of my handsome ex, I find a punchy middle-aged man.

Flustered, I grab the closest snack I find and bring it to the counter. Mom will be suspicious if I come out empty-handed. The man rings up the purchase and takes my money, hardly giving me a glance.

Mom is playing with the radio dial when I return.

"We can listen to music now?" I ask, buckling my seat belt.

"I think it's safe to allow it." She looks at the bag in my hand. "You haven't had those in a long time."

For the first time I focus on what I bought. A single-serving bag of Doritos. They used to be my favorite.

"Don't eat them, Fatty. Treatment bloated you like a greedy boy on Thanksgiving."

I pull the bag open and get a waft of fresh, cheesy scented Doritos. Instead of arguing with Anna, I shove a whole chip into my mouth and crunch.

Mom's right—it's been a long time since I ate a Dorito. I used to beg her to buy them for me as a kid, but she didn't often because she was sure one of the ingredients could cause cancer. When I started to restrict food, though, she no longer cared about what I ate.

Swallowing the Dorito is amazing. I allow myself to enjoy the taste, texture, and mental relief at eating something that WHT would classify as my "fear foods"—foods I'd typically restrict because of the anxiety. There are a few other foods I haven't been able to bring myself to eat though. This is the first time since exiting WHT that I've been able to enjoy a fear food. Does that mean Anna's grip is getting looser, or that I'm having a normal girl moment?

I'm not sure, but I like this small amount of freedom. I didn't see Jax like I wanted to, but maybe it's better this way. Now I don't have to wallow in sadness, knowing he has a girlfriend when I only have Hope and my mom. Dad is never in the picture long enough to be considered "there for me." I'll have to ask Hope to bring me to the gas station again. Once I get my driver's license then I can go wherever I want. Well, once I get a car, of course—but I don't doubt that Dad will buy me one in an effort to make up for his guilt.

Now I just need to pass the test. Only two more months.

Chapter 10

F*riday, September 8th, 2017*

8:30 AM

Home

I hauled my duffel bag that was filled with clothes, blankets, chargers, batteries, and electronic devices to the front door. I even packed a manila envelope that was filled with printed pictures I didn't want to lose, just in case the house flooded or blew off the earth like the house did in the movie, *Up.* I also wedged one of my favorite kaleidoscopes into my purse. The tube was teal and silver, striped with gold sequins. A small part of me was intimidated by the doom reports that were announced on the news regarding the hurricane, and I wanted this one piece of my collection in case we lost the house.

Mom's suitcase was already set by the front door.

"Ariel?"

I followed her voice to her bedroom and found her struggling with the king-sized mattress that she and my dad had shared.

"Will you help me cover the windows with this?"

I grabbed the bed and tried to move the thing, which must have weighed more than ten dead bodies. "Why didn't you hire someone to board up the windows like Grandma did?"

Mom grunted as she strained to move the mattress. "I tried, but the man said he had too many houses to do already. I told your dad we'd do what we could."

We struggled with the mattress but were only able to shove it off the twin box springs. Mom set her hands on her hips and sighed. "I guess we'll have to use the box springs instead. There's no way we'll get that mattress against the windows." We moved the much-lighter box springs over the windows. "Speaking of your Dad, he's going to try to come home today."

The news caused me to hesitate for a moment. "Can he make it? Would he stay with us at Grandma's house, or would we stay here?"

"We'd stay with your grandma. She has the shutters."

"Why is he coming?" Mom walked into the living room. "You asked him to, didn't you?"

She removed a glass vase from the TV stand and brought it to the closet. "We should move things like this to keep them from breaking or falling if we lose the windows."

"Mom," I prodded. "Did you ask him to come home?" Mom wasn't the kind of woman to ask for help or even to react in fear. If she asked Dad to come home, then this hurricane was a bigger deal to her than she made it out to be. She kept downplaying the storm with words, but then she turned around and asked Dad to come home? She wouldn't do that unless she was scared.

She found a spot for the vase and shut the closet door. "Yes." The admission froze me in place. My strong mom—the one who loved Florida and wasn't afraid of anything—had asked my dad to come home because this storm scared her. "I couldn't get your grandma to evacuate, and it's better for you to stay close in case a bed opens up, so I asked him to come home."

I almost asked, *what in the world could my business-minded aloof dad do to help in a situation like this?* But I thought better of it. The comfort of having him with us would ease my misgivings about the storm too. There's something hardwired in our brains that acknowledges that our dads are supposed to be there for us. He put work before us, but I still hoped one day he'd choose Mom and me.

"I'm going to get the gas can from the garage and put it in the trunk. I don't think your grandma has extra gas for the generator. Can you finish clearing the living room?"

"Sure."

Mom and I continued to take safety precautions in the house. We emptied the kitchen counters of all appliances, cups, and other objects that could transform into projectiles during strong winds. We also moved all of the porch furniture into the garage and removed picture frames and vases from our tables.

By the time we were ready to go to Grandma's, our house was empty. It almost looked as though a hurricane had already ripped through it and moved all of our possessions from their places.

12:00 PM

Grandma's house

Grandma's house smelled like freshly baked brownies. I found her standing at the kitchen counter doing a crossword puzzle. The digital numbers on her stove ticked down the time until the brownies would be done.

"Grandma, wouldn't you rather sit?"

She slid her pencil behind her ear like a construction

worker. "I used to be a runner. Sitting all day makes my butt fat."

I shook my head in amusement. "You look fine." And for a seventy-eight-year-old woman, she did. Old people weren't supposed to be slim and fit. They could let themselves go—but Grandma still power walked the neighborhood when she could.

Mom rolled her suitcase into the spare bedroom. "Ariel, do you want the bed or the air mattress?"

Why was she giving me the option? I would look selfish if I chose the bed. "I'll sleep on the air mattress. You and dad can have the bed."

Grandma jerked her gaze toward me. "Jeremy's coming? I thought he was in Boston."

Mom came out of the bedroom, heading toward the small laundry room. "Air mattress is in here, right?"

"Caroline Mary." Grandma didn't call my mom by her first and middle name often, but when she did, it meant she had something to say.

Mom halted and switched directions. She stopped at the kitchen counter. "Yes, Mom?"

"Jeremy's coming?"

"Yes."

Grandma retrieved the pencil from behind her ear and dropped it on top of her puzzle. "Why?" It wasn't the first time in my life that I got the impression Grandma didn't like Dad.

Mom stood her ground. "Because I asked him to."

The timer on the oven beeped, and Grandma turned to rescue her brownies from burning. Mom used the distraction as an escape. "Air mattress is in the laundry room, right, Mom?"

I relaxed into the warmth that flooded the kitchen as Grandma opened the oven door. She set the brownies on the stove and switched the oven off.

Mom entered the kitchen seconds later. "I can't find the air mattress."

"It's in the garage. When you come back, can you bring me two frozen bananas from the freezer out there?"

"Sure. I'll get the gas can from the car and put it with the generator."

"Caroline."

Mom turned at the change in her voice. "Yes?"

"I don't have a generator anymore."

Mom blinked rapidly in surprise as she took in the news. "What do you mean? Where did it go?"

"We haven't had a big hurricane in a while, and a family at church was having power issues, so I gave it to them almost six years ago."

Mom took on the form of a statue. Just seconds earlier she had thought we were prepared to brave Irma. "What will we do if the power goes out?"

Grandma swept her hand around the kitchen. "I'm going to make enough food to last us a week or two. I'm making banana bread next. I'll keep it in the freezer until the power goes out. Then I'll make granola bars and homemade bread for peanut butter and jelly sandwiches. Hate to break it to ya, but those pitas you got are just awful. But we'll have plenty of food, so don't worry."

"But . . ." Mom couldn't seem to formulate a complete thought. Then she must have had an idea, because her worry lines left as she finally took a breath. "I completely forgot. We have a generator at the house in Lakeland. It's in the shed."

The house was located in central Florida, an hour southwest of our home in Orlando. It was Mom and Dad's second house, one that Dad had inherited from his parents. The beautiful, remodeled home sat on Lake Hollingsworth. We used to vacation there in the summer—but when Dad's business grew, we started to use it less and less. Now he had it listed it as an Airbnb.

Grandma pulled out a large bowl and two bread pans from a cupboard. "Oh, there's no need to drive out there and get it. We'll be just fine without it."

"I'd feel better if we had a generator," Mom said.

"If you want to waste your time and gas money, then fine. But I don't need it."

Mom frowned at Grandma. "Jeremy and I can go tomorrow."

Grandma ignored her.

"I'll get your bananas." Mom spun around and headed toward the garage.

2:45 PM

Grandma's house

The war in my head started when the aroma of banana bread leaked out from the edges of the oven and mixed with the already-sweet scent of chocolate. Grandma shuffled around the kitchen while Mom busied herself by making up the bed, air mattress, and sorting clothes into dresser drawers.

I want a slice of hot, melt-in-your-mouth banana bread.

"Do you know how many calories are in banana bread?" Anna said. "It's like eating a muffin—which is like eating a cupcake without the frosting. Eating a slice of banana bread would hurt you the same way that eating a slice of cake would. You don't need anything else to help you become more unattractive than you already are. Treatment is going to pack the pounds on you, so why start now?"

But shouldn't I start stretching my stomach now? These calories won't count because I'll be eating a lot more at treatment. One slice is nothing compared to what I'll be eating in a few days.

"Maybe you can avoid treatment."

How?

"Convince them you aren't sick enough."

They wanted to admit me to the hospital. There's no way I can pass for healthy enough to ditch treatment. I'd have to gain weight, and to do that I'd have to eat more. Such as this banana bread.

"You're weak."

I watched a TV show on my iPhone to keep the war from spilling onto my facial expressions. Grandma and Mom would be worried if they knew how much I fought to keep myself under control, how much of a fight it was for me to live in my own skin.

Minutes later, Grandma used floral oven mitts to pull two bread pans out of the oven. She left them on the stove to cool and moved on to her next project. Homemade granola bars.

Steam rose from the bread like mist off water on a cool day. My mouth watered at the sight and scent. I turned my attention back to my phone, determined not to think about food. Which wasn't easy—especially since I sat at the kitchen counter while Grandma mixed oatmeal, honey, dark chocolate, dried cherries, cinnamon, and other ingredients to make her gooey bars. Chocolate, bananas, and now cinnamon tested my willpower as their fragrances mixed and filled the house with a sweet fragrance.

I should go outside and remove myself from the temptation.

Grandma slid a knife along the interior edges of the bread pans, then she flipped them over, careful to extract the bread in whole pieces. She sawed her bread knife through the larger loaf until a pile of bread slices fell onto the cutting board like edible dominoes.

Grandma placed two slices onto a china tea plate and then slid it across the table toward me. She didn't ask if I was hungry.

I set my phone down, my show forgotten. Like a dog with a new bone, I wanted to take this offering to a private place where I could devour it. "Mind if I bring this outside to the garden?"

"Of course, darling," she said.

I took the plate and scurried to Grandma's backyard. A fence kept her space private from her neighbors—but instead of a lanai and pool, her backyard was filled with flowers. They started at the fence and grew inward. A path of green grass ran through the yard, flowers and herbs planted every few feet. A bench faced the man-made pond, which was the size of a coffee table.

I slipped my shoes and socks off, then walked across the fresh green carpet of earth, toward the bench. Instead of sitting on the ground, I found a spot near the pond and leaned my back against the wooden bench. Soft grass tickled my legs as the sun warmed the wooden bench, heating my back. I set the china plate on my thighs, studying the bread that was filled with brown flecks of cooked banana.

I'll only eat one of the two pieces.

"You shouldn't eat any of it, Fatty."

None of this matters because of the hurricane. Who cares what I eat if I'm about to die anyway? Some news reporters are making it sound like the apocalypse is coming. One—or two—pieces of banana bread are not going to make or break my world.

"Don't eat it."

I want to.

"Don't.

Before I could argue back, I snatched a slice of bread and took a huge bite. The taste filled my mouth and quickly turned to dough with my fast-working jaw.

I swallowed and took another ravenous bite—but panic stopped me from taking another. What was I doing? I couldn't eat this. But I wanted to.

I chewed once and twice more. Then, without thinking, I jerked my head to the side and spit the food into the pond. The motion was like a reflex.

I raked my teeth over my tongue and spit the crumbs out too. I couldn't eat it. I couldn't. *But I wanted to.*

What was wrong with me?

I lifted the bread to my mouth, preparing to take another bite—but I couldn't force my lips to part. I leaned over the pond and heaved deep breaths. It was like my body couldn't decide if it wanted to throw up, have a panic attack, pass out, or scream.

My jaw quivered as I caught sight of my reflection in the still water. Bits of regurgitated food floated above the reflection of my head like a cloud. I ground my teeth at the sight of my confused, flushed, and terror-stricken face. I almost didn't recognize the angles of my cheeks or the orbs of my eyes.

Anna didn't appear beside me. In that moment, I could only see myself.

I didn't *look* like myself though. No ripples marred the water, but I didn't need them for my face to look distorted. I couldn't help the thought that speared me at the mirror image.

Who am I?

Anna didn't answer. She couldn't. My question went deeper than her shallow existence.

I looked at the bits of food again. Shame filled me, and I slapped my hand against the surface of the water in a surge of rage. My image fragmented with the water's disturbance.

I lifted my head toward the blue sky and groaned deep in my throat, clutching the sides of my head. I was so broken that I couldn't even recognize myself. The weight of the china and second slice of bread that rested on my thighs felt like a semi truck.

I hefted the bread off the plate, stood, stumbled, and threw it like a professional baseball player would throw a ball. It crumpled and dissipated over the flowers and grass before it could splatter against the wooden fence.

The plate had rolled toward the edge of the pond, but it

didn't slip in. I rested my hands on my knees and breathed in deep, trying to regain control of myself.

The grass between my feet blurred to match the pattern of a kaleidoscope. Blinking, I allowed myself to fall forward. I caught myself on my palms and crumpled to the earth. Grass met my cheek as I cried.

I couldn't do this. I couldn't eat. I no longer knew how to stay alive.

"Ariel?"

I sat up at Grandma's voice and wiped the tears off my face.

"You out here?" Her voice came from the sliding glass door that was attached to the living room.

"Yes, Grandma." I made my voice sound as cheerful and normal as possible.

"Did you like the bread?"

I forced myself to keep from looking at the pond, where the pieces of bread still floated. "Yeah. It was—great."

"Glad you liked it. Come on inside for a bit. The granola bars are ready."

"Thanks. Be there in a little while."

As soon as I heard the sliding door close, I collapsed back onto the grass. I had to pull myself together before I went back inside. Mom would expect me to eat something for dinner, and I had to pretend that I was okay. I had to fake it.

At least until I could fall apart in treatment.

5:00 PM

Grandma's house

Since Grandma was in the kitchen all day, she allowed Mom to make our dinner. I'd dried my tears and resumed my seat at the kitchen counter at a cushioned bar stool, using my phone for entertainment purposes. Mom chopped lettuce to make a salad, and a huge pan of chicken and broccoli casserole baked in the oven.

"When will Dad arrive?" I asked. Mom hadn't mentioned him the rest of the day, and neither Grandma nor myself asked.

She didn't turn from her chopping. "I don't know."

The lack of communication didn't surprise me. Mom had probably tried to call, and he didn't answer. "Will you need to pick him up from the airport? When does his plane land?"

Mom repeated herself. "I don't know."

Grandma huffed from the living room, obviously eaves-dropping on our conversation.

"Have you tried calling him?"

She shrugged. "No."

"When was the last time you talked to him?" I asked.

"He texted me this morning."

"You'd better find out what's going on. I'm not waiting up all night for him to get here," Grandma said.

Mom stopped chopping, looked to the ceiling, and sighed. "Fine. Ariel, come here. Get my phone out of my back pocket."

I slipped the phone from her jeans and returned to my seat. "Want me to call?"

"Yes. Just get the details."

I found Dad's number, pressed the call button, and then put it on speakerphone. It'd be helpful for all of us to hear him.

But looking back, I wish I hadn't.

The phone rang four times before connecting. "Hello?"

A female's voice.

I should have been more surprised, but I knew my dad. Another girl might have been shocked to hear a strange woman answer her dad's phone. But not me. In retrospect, this must have been what Mom had feared, the reason she didn't call Dad all day. I figured he'd cheated on Mom, and I think Mom knew, too—but this was the first time either of us had received confirmation.

Regaining my composure, I answered, "Is—is Jeremy there?" My dad's name felt strange on my tongue.

"Yes. Who is this?" The woman sounded annoyed.

My brows shot up as my eyes widened. I didn't look over my shoulder to see Grandma's expression, but Mom had turned from her cutting board to stare at the phone. Her lips parted with a slow intake of breath. Her eyes closed like lazy elevator doors as she absorbed the unwanted trajectory of her life.

Anger buffeted my chest, and I spat the first words that came to mind. "I'm his daughter."

The woman had the audacity to say, "Oh, snap." Only, instead of saying snap, she chose a more colorful word.

I heard a shuffle. Then, "Jer, it's for you."

She called him *Jer*? Mom didn't even call him that. My dad's voice sounded distant. "Who is it? What? Why are you—" A few crackles, and then, "Hello? Who is this?"

Mom flashed her eyes open. She gripped the edge of the granite counter, leaned over the phone, and said, "Hello, Jeremy."

The voices of newscasters on the TV were the only sound in the room as we waited for Dad's response.

He finally answered with one word. "Caroline." But there was no remorse or bewilderment in his voice—only a flat, expressionless tone.

I couldn't help myself. "Are you coming home?" I asked.

There was a soft curse on the other end of the line. "Ariel, what . . . am I on speakerphone?"

"You sure are," Grandma yelled from the couch.

Dad groaned. "Ariel, I'm sorry. I can't make it."

"Did you even try?" I shot back.

His lack of response was all the answer I needed.

Mom took the phone in her hand. "Don't come back, Jeremy." And then she hung up.

We shared glances as the TV droned in the background.

The timer on the oven beeped. Mom dropped the phone and pivoted toward the oven. She used the same floral mitts that Grandma had used for baking and extracted the casserole. Her chopped vegetables were left forgotten on the counter.

After setting the casserole down on top of the stove, she whirled around. "Excuse me," she said, then hurried away toward the bedrooms.

Grandma shook her head and clicked her tongue. "I had a feeling about him from the very beginning. The only blessing that came out of their relationship was you." She spoke like they were already divorced.

I swiveled the bar stool toward the living room. "What do you think will happen?"

Grandma pinched her lips together. "I don't know, darling. I just don't know." She walked in the direction Mom disappeared, probably to comfort her.

A memory tried to resurface, but I pushed it back down. Dad's infidelity was not unexpected from any of us, but it still hurt. I'd never forget the silence that came from the other end of the phone after I'd asked if he had tried to come home.

He didn't.

A life-threatening hurricane was headed toward Florida, and he didn't care enough about his own wife and daughter to come home and protect us.

A light on the stove caught my attention. I stood to turn the oven off and hovered over the casserole. Should we eat without Mom, or was this my chance to get out of dinner?

Remembering my internal struggle in the garden, I backed away from the food, afraid to eat even a carrot off of the cutting board. I didn't mean to spit the food out. It was a compulsion. I didn't want to die, but I didn't necessarily want to eat, either.

As I looked at the oven, I remembered Mom's plan to retrieve the generator the next day with Dad. Would she still go? Irma was probably becoming the accompaniment to the hurt in her heart—dark, swirling emotions, and the threat of permanent damage.

But it wasn't just Mom's life that resembled the hurricane. It was mine too. Only my life carried with it the fear of death. I swirled between Anna and reason like the bands of wind whipping around the eye of the hurricane. I was already living in the darkness, the swirl of emotions, and the damage caused by my eating disorder.

Attempting to evacuate Florida would be like attempting to escape the hurricane of my eating disorder.

Impossible. Useless to even try.

Chapter 11

P*resent*
   February 22nd, 2018

HOPE IS MORE than happy to stop at the gas station after school.
I haven't looked for Jax since the day Mom and I practiced
driving.

Hope pulls into the parking lot, and my heart beats as fast
as though I just ran a 5K. I need to ask Jax what he regrets
about us.

"I'll wait here," she says. "Good luck."

"Hopefully he'll be here."

I get out of the car and slam the door behind me. I've spent
days trying to work up the courage to walk through these doors
again.

I enter and scan the store. Anticipation increases the pace
of my heart, so much that it feels like it's stuttering in my chest.

And then I see him. He stands behind the counter before a
line of customers. I hide in the candy aisle and wait. Every few
seconds, I peek over the aisle to see if the line has shrunk.

Soon the customers have left and it's only the two of us. I straighten my shoulders, take a deep breath to calm myself, and round the aisle.

He glances up and raises his eyebrows. "Ariel?" He notices my empty hands. "Are you buying anything?"

That's what he wants to know? If I'm buying anything? I don't even get a *hello*?

I cross my arms. "I came to talk to you."

He cocks his head to the side like an interested dog.

"I—"

The bell above the door rings, and three girls walk inside.

I take a step back. "I'll wait over here." I gesture over my shoulder.

"Wait. You don't have to—"

But I dart back to the candy aisle. The girls take their time choosing snacks and drinks to buy. When they finally leave, I've nearly worked myself into a panic attack.

Jax finds me staring at chocolates and sucking air through my lips like a straw. "You okay there?"

I try not to act like an idiot as I face him. "I came to—"

The bell rings again. I'm tempted to run out the door as it swings shut behind a new customer. "I'll just go."

His fingers wrap around my arm in a gentle grip before I can dash out. "Come," he says, then leads me toward a room behind the cash counter. He sets me in a red metal folding chair. "Are you okay being in here while I help this guy? We can talk when he leaves."

"Yeah. Sure. Okay." I sound like a stuttering parrot.

I send a text to Hope after Jax leaves.

Me: *He's here. Give me a few minutes.*

. . .

SHE RESPONDS with a thumbs up emoji, as well as a kissy face.

When the bell rings, signaling an exit, Jax appears in the doorway. "Sorry about that." He rests his shoulder against the doorframe. "So," he says. "You came to see me."

"I did."

He studies me. "What for?"

"To talk."

"About?"

"Last time."

His endearing, too-big smile widens on his face. "I need more than two words at a time please."

"Oh. Sorry."

"That's two words, Ariel."

I slap my palm against my forehead.

"Are you nervous? You don't have to be afraid to talk to me."

"I want to know what it is that you regret," I blurt out.

He pushes away from the doorframe, and I can tell he's confused. "What are you talking about?"

"When I saw you here last, you were about to say that you regretted something. It's been bothering me ever since." The words spill out as I grip the seat of my chair.

"I—" The bell chimes again. He holds up his index finger. "Hold that thought."

I want to groan at the interruption, but instead, I release my claw-like grip from the chair and force myself to set my hands in my lap.

Jax comes back five minutes later. "Sorry. That's gonna keep happening." He checks his phone. "My shift is over in an hour. Want to hang in here and we can talk in my car afterwards?"

I shrug as if it's not a big deal. "Sure."

As soon as he leaves, I give Hope a call. "He wants me to stay and talk after his shift. Can you pick me up in two hours? That should give us enough time."

"Ummm . . . I've got homework, but I could probably swing by again. What will you tell your mom?"

"She's at Grandma's house and won't be home until later. She won't notice."

"So you sure you're good?"

"Yeah," I whisper. "He doesn't seem mad."

"All right. Well, don't get into any trouble."

"Very funny."

After we end the call, I kill time in the break room by scrolling through my social media accounts and checking my email. When Jax is finally done, he passes the shift to the next guy and then the two of us head outside together.

The sight of his small Honda SUV makes my heart flutter. The last time I sat in that front seat was not my finest or clear headed moment.

Jax must be thinking along the same lines. "Would you rather sit on the hood and talk?"

"No. It's okay."

When we're both settled in the car, he picks up from where we left off. "So you came back to ask me what I regret?"

I pick at what appears to be a melted Starburst taffy on his fabric seat. "When I saw you last, you were about to tell me that you regretted something—and then you got cut off. I was too much of a chicken to stick around and hear you out."

"And you're not chicken now?" A smirk rises on his lips.

I flick the pink taffy onto the floor. "I'm trying not to be."

Jax reaches toward me, but then draws his hand back. "You don't have to be afraid of me."

I quirk my brow. Was he going to take my hand? "I've never been afraid of you. It's more like—anxiety. A fear of what you'll say, not a fear of you as a person."

Why am I being so honest with him?

"That makes me feel a little better, but you should know I'd never do anything to hurt you."

"I know." And I do. He's Jax. Enough said.

He sighs and wraps his arm around the headrest of his seat, his chest now fully facing me. His red polo shirt that he wears for work looks weird on him. I'm used to seeing him wear T-shirts. "I don't remember our last conversation exactly. I was just surprised to see you. But what I regret about our relation-ship—is that what you wanna know?"

"Yes. Please."

He takes his time thinking. "Okay, but promise that you won't judge."

"Why would I judge you? I'm the one who—"

"Just listen, Ariel."

I force my mouth shut.

He glances out the windshield, then back at me. "I regret not trying harder. I should have contacted you. I didn't know how to help, and I took our breakup personally—even though I was pretty sure it had something to do with your illness. But here you are, better—and now I feel like a jerk for not at least *attempting* to still be your friend. Then, once I turned eighteen, Mom stopped getting child support checks for me. I had to get a job and start college classes . . . I know those are a lot of excuses. But the bottom line, Ariel, is—I regret that I didn't try harder."

I open my mouth, but nothing comes out.

"I'm sorry," he says.

I shake my head in slow motion. "It was never about you, Jax."

"That's nice to know."

"It was always me. I was the one who was sick. And I'm still not completely better, but at least I'm seeing a counselor now. I'm trying."

"You look great."

I squeeze my eyes tight. "Please, don't say that. I know you think it's nice, but I'm not ready to hear it." Although I know he meant it as a compliment my brain heard, *"You look fat."* Because if I look great it means I don't look anorexic which means I gained weight.

He gives a quick nod. "Yes, sorry. I didn't know. See? I don't know how to . . . deal with you. I wanted to, and I should have at least tried." He grimaces. "Wait, I didn't mean *deal* with you. I meant—ah. I'm going to shut up now."

Deal with me? I want to argue, but I can't—because he's right. I was so sick the last time I saw him. Friends and family had to walk on thin ice just to navigate simple conversations with me.

Jax reaches out and takes my hand. "So—what now?"

Why is he holding my hand? I broke his heart. Crushed it to pieces. I don't deserve his kindness.

I observe our interlaced fingers, not knowing if I like it or am terrified by the idea of us being more than friends again. How could he consider being with me after the way I pushed him away? Or is he just being nice in an attempt to comfort me?

I don't know if I can handle a relationship, and I really don't want to hurt him again.

I guide his hand back to his side of the car, breaking apart his hold. "I could honestly use another friend."

Jax doesn't seem offended by the friend card. "You tell me what you need, and I'll be there for you."

He is making this way too easy. I expected some sort of admonishment for the way I ended things.

"No one is going to mind if you . . . you know. Text a different girl?"

He looks like he wants to reach for me again, but he refrains himself. "Ariel, there's been no one since you."

My jaw drops.

He shrugs one shoulder, "No time."

I check the digital clock that flashes on the dashboard.

"Sorry, but I should go. I didn't tell Mom that I'd be here, and I need to text Hope. She's picking me up."

"You don't have a driver's license yet?"

I give him a dull look. "I was too sick when I was sixteen, and I turned seventeen while I was in treatment. I've only been out for a few months."

He raises his hands in surrender. "Okay, okay. Sorry I asked." He thinks for a moment, then says, "Why don't I take you home?"

I consider his offer. It would be nice to not have to bother Hope. It wouldn't hurt to accept, would it?

"Fine."

Jax starts the car as I text Hope to inform her about the change in plans.

Neither of us talk on the drive. I want to ask him more about his life, but I can't seem to wrap my head around his apology. *I* should be the one apologizing. Not him.

Jax parks the car at the curb and leans back in his seat. "Can I give you a hug?"

Ignoring his question, I unbuckle. "Why are you being nice after the way I pushed you away?"

He fiddles with the lock button on his door handle. "Because I blame myself too. Like I said before, I should have tried harder to stay with you. I promised I'd wait, and then . . ."

Glancing at my house, I allow my gaze to travel beyond, in the direction of the park—where we met on Labor Day. I wouldn't have guessed that I'd be talking to Jax again when I started to write in the journal. But now, here we are.

I bite my bottom lip and rest my hand on his arm. "Jax, I am so sorry. I thought I was doing what was best for you. I thought I was right. These past few months have been hard, and being in a relationship would have made them much harder."

The way his face darkens with sadness tells me that he doesn't understand. "But I could have helped. I wanted to help."

"I know. But I needed to be healthy on my own before I could be in a relationship."

His eyes brighten. "Are you saying you want to get back together?"

That escalated quickly. "What? No, I just wanted to talk. I— I'm not . . ." I release my hold on his arm, struggling for words.

Jax laughs. "I was just curious."

"I meant it when I said I just wanted to be friends. I'm still working through some personal issues." I think about the journal and the fights I've had with Anna recently.

Jax nods slowly, like he's agreeing with me even though he doesn't want to. "Can I hug you?" he asks again.

It's cute how he's acting. Almost as if he's been waiting for me this whole time—just waiting for me to show up at the gas station and find him.

"Yes," I say.

Jax scooches closer until he can wrap his arms around me. I can smell the faint scent of his cologne beneath the reek of gasoline and gas station food.

"I'm so sorry, Ariel. I've been a jerk. I should have—"

"Stop." I pull away. "Let's just start over, okay? As friends."

His lips tilt into a half-smile. "Friends," he agrees.

I slide out of the car and wave as Jax drives away. I guess my ex-boyfriend just became my friend again. I wonder what our relationship will look like this time around.

Chapter 12

Saturday, September 9th, 2017

7:30 AM

Grandma's house

Voices woke me from my shelter I'd created between the cotton sheets and fluffy white comforter. I slept on the air mattress in the living room while Mom took the second bedroom. Alone.

"Mom, how long have you been like this?" I heard my mom ask. "Why didn't you call me?"

Grandma's voice was muffled, but I made out the words. "I'm fine, Caroline. Just help me up and stop fussing."

Shuffles, and then Mom's voice again. "Are you okay?"

"Yes, yes." Grandma sounded embarrassed. What could they have been talking about? I ground my teeth, took a deep breath, and threw the sheets off me. The shock of cold air made me want to hibernate back between the covers, but I slipped on fluffy socks and followed the voices into the hallway and toward Grandma's suite.

I padded through her room and into the bathroom. Mom had Grandma propped onto a stool. They both looked at me as I entered.

"What's going on?"

Grandma waved me off. "Nothing. Caroline was just leaving. I'm about to take a shower."

Mom studied Grandma, her eyes roving over her body. She stopped at her ankle. "Mom, you twisted your ankle. I should bring you in."

The powder pink and white accented room looked like it came out of a two decade old TV show. Grandma winced when she tried to stand.

"How long have you been lying on the floor?" Mom asked, then she looked at me. "I came to check on her and found her lying here." She pointed at the rug by the shower. "She's too stubborn to let me help."

"I don't *need* help," Grandma argued.

"Not according to your green and blue-colored ankle," Mom said. "You need to get X-rays done." She forced her hair back in a loose bun at the base of her neck. "Great. Now I can't get the generator," she said to herself. She focused on Grandma again. "Come on. I'll help you get dressed."

Grandma tested weight on her ankle. She winced and fell backwards onto the stool. "It's not broken."

"How do you know?"

She glared at Mom. "I know my body, Caroline. I've been alive a lot longer than you."

"I'm taking you to emergency."

I stood in the doorway, unsure of whose side to take. Realizing I'd be of no help to either of them, I left the room to get dressed.

Morning light seeped through the curtains in the living

room, making it easy to find the clothes I'd set out the night before. I dressed in the middle of the room, then I went back into the bathroom.

Mom's shoulder was placed beneath Grandma's arm as she led her toward the bedroom. I supported her other arm, helping them to Grandma's bed.

"Are you going out?" I said.

Mom gave Grandma a pointed look, and Grandma gave her own stare back in return. She lifted her leg and studied the bruised ankle. "It'll heal on its own in a few days. No big deal."

Mom snapped. Her emotions were hot—probably sparked when she discovered that Dad was cheating. "You need to stop being a stubborn old woman and—"

"What more do you expect?" Grandma cut in. "Like it or not, I *am* a stubborn old woman. And you are a stubborn *girl.* So leave me be."

"Fine. Have it your way." Mom threw her hands in the air and stomped out of the room. I gave Grandma an apologetic shrug then followed Mom.

I found her in the second bedroom, rummaging through a drawer of clothes. Tears streaked her cheeks. Moms weren't supposed to cry—but in one week, she'd fought for her daughter's life, discovered her husband was cheating, and now her mother was injured. And she was powerless to help or fix any of us.

I faltered in the doorway. "Are you okay?"

Mom wouldn't look at me.

Should I go?

She snatched a shirt out of the drawer and then slammed the dresser shut.

"I'm sorry to bother you," I said. "I'll go."

Before I could leave, Mom rushed forward and reached for my hand. "No, Ariel. Stay." She pulled me to her chest, holding me tight. I could smell the vanilla lotion she used before bed on her skin. Her wet cheek met mine. We were the same height. "I love you so much," she said.

I hugged her back, unwilling to leave her tight embrace. For years, we'd been a family of three—although Dad only hovered along the sidelines. Now, though, we were a family of two. A family of damaged souls who were trying to hang on to any shreds of normalcy in our lives. We had Grandma, but something must have shifted with the phone call the day before.

"I love you too, Mom." I couldn't imagine anything more comforting than allowing Mom to hold me. "What are you going to do?"

She released me and wiped her cheeks with her palms. "I'm sorry you had to see me like this."

"It's okay." In the last week, I'd seen my mom in a warmer light. Moms were supposed to be our strong protectors and nurturers—at least, that's what I had always assumed. But seeing the tears in her eyes as her life fell apart, I began to view her differently. Not just as my mother, but as a grown-up girl who—like myself—was struggling to navigate this crazy world.

She fanned her face, drying the tear tracks. "I'm going to take your grandma to the hospital for X-rays. I know we fight sometimes but we really do love each other. I hope she didn't break anything."

"I know," I said. Then I stated the obvious. "But she doesn't want to go."

Mom forced a smile. "She's the cripple in this situation, so she doesn't exactly have a choice. Let me get dressed, and then I'll take care of her. You can stay here."

Mom left me in the bedroom as she went to change in grandma's room.

I stood in the middle of the room and looked at the unmade bed, empty suitcases, and drawn curtains. In effort to help Mom, I decided to open the curtains, make the bed, and stow the suitcases into the closet. What else could I do to pitch in?

An idea that came to me made me pause midstep. Mom wanted the generator. She'd be ecstatic if she came home from the hospital to find it in the garage in time for the hurricane. The lake house was only an hour away. But how could I get there without a driver's license?

Determination released adrenaline into my veins. I was struggling, and Dad broke Mom's heart—but at least the generator could make her smile. If I could surprise her with this, it would be like setting a stray puzzle piece of her life back into its rightful place.

But how?

A Cheshire-cat smile spread across my face. I found my phone and called Hope.

12:20 PM

Hope's car

The song "Despacito" had me dancing in my seat as Hope and I drove an hour southwest, headed toward Lakeland, Florida. She volunteered to come right away, although she *did* have to lie to her parents, convincing them that she was spending time at Grandma's with me. But after telling her about last night's phone call, we both agreed that the lie would be worth the reward.

There weren't many people on the roads. We passed a few road construction sites that had orange cones but no workers. Schools were closed through Monday, and many Florida residents had evacuated, or they were in the process of doing so. We drove south, although most people were driving *north*. The windows were rolled down, and the dial on the radio was twisted as far as it could go.

Irma may have been upon us, but we still had a whole hour of pure freedom. There was something about warm air blowing hair across my face as I listened to upbeat music that made me feel alive.

I remember this moment vividly—mainly because I haven't felt the same reckless freedom since then. It's crazy to think how, at a time so catastrophic, I somehow managed to find a few minutes of peace. It was the kind of peace and freedom that no one could have taken away from me.

Not even Anna.

1:00 PM

Lake house

I examined the houses bordering Lake Hollingsworth as Hope and I neared the lake house. Sandbags were piled in some of their front yards or against their doors. Less expensive homes that were further from the road used tape or cardboard across their windows. A handful of the homes used hurricane shutters, but just as many didn't. In the distance, the steeple of a white church rose above the trees.

Hope pulled into the driveway at around one in the afternoon. The driveway sat behind the house. As soon as she parked, I jumped out of the car and ran around to see the water. I crossed the street and stopped on the edge. An old dock stretched into the lake like the setting of a romance film. It wasn't a great place for swimming because alligators could lurk almost anywhere, but the lake was used for recreational activities, such as water skiing, sailing, kayaking, and canoeing.

Hope stood beside me. "I've only been here once. It's beautiful."

"This is one of my favorite places. I wish we came here more. I'd bring you along, but I'm not sure what will happen now that . . ."

I couldn't think too hard about what life would look like

since my dad's infidelity had been brought to light. Instead, I watched the water shimmer as it basked in the sunshine.

After a moment, I took Hope's hand and led her back toward the street. "Let's get the generator and go home. I want to have it at Grandma's before they get back from the hospital."

We rounded the house, passed the car, and stopped in front of the shed. Dad had built it a few years ago to house lawn equipment because the lake house didn't have a garage.

I found the key in a fake rock and unlocked the door. Hope and I crowded into the tight space, which smelled like dank air, and I scanned the room. Lawn mowers, hedge trimmers, beach chairs, kayaks, and other vacation items were crammed into the small space. Dust floated around the room.

Then I spotted it. "There." I pointed toward the back wall where the generator sat.

Disappointment weighted my limbs. It was bigger than I'd remembered—about the size of a grill, only shorter and stouter.

We wound through the obstacle course of items and reached the generator. The now-empty tank could hold up to seven gallons of gas. I ran my finger along the dusty metal frame.

"Ummm . . ."

"Uh-huh." I knew we were thinking the same thing.

There was no way we could get the generator home.

I crouched and tested my next theory by wrapping my hands around the frame, using my legs to lift with all my might. It didn't budge a millimeter. Hope crouched into the same maneuver and grunted as she used all her strength to try and move the machine. She only succeeded in moving it an inch.

She winced at me. "Sorry, but I don't think we can do it."

I stared at the generator, trying to think of something we could do, some way we could move it.

I scanned the shed for a tool that might help, but there was none.

Moaning, I kicked the beast of a generator with a silent curse at its immovability.

Hope placed a hand on my arm and guided me away. "We should go. We tried. Maybe that will cheer your mom up?"

I kicked the unmovable metal traitor once more before making my way through the maze and back toward the door. "No. She'd be mad I came without permission."

"No joke. We need to get home before my parents realize I lied about where I was going." Hope waited as I locked the doors and hid the key back in the rock.

Back at the car, I said, "I guess we have no choice but to stick out this stupid hurricane without power. If I'm lucky, they'll let me into treatment on Monday or Tuesday. I bet they'll get power before we do, and even if they don't, they still have generators."

"You want to go to treatment now? I thought you were only tolerating the idea."

"I—"

Hope cut me off with the first swear word I had ever heard her utter.

I halted in bewilderment. "What?"

Hope stopped with furrowed brow, mouth twisted in astonishment, and eyes wide. I followed her gaze to her red hatchback and gasped. The whole car slumped to the rear left where the rim of her tire kissed the dirt.

"Crap. We must have hit a nail or something when we went through the construction sites," I tried to rally. "I've never changed a tire before, but we can figure it out. We have the Internet, after all. This happened to you recently, didn't it? You know how to do it, right?"

She didn't move. Her jaw now gapped open as she stood frozen.

I waved a hand in front of her face. "It's not a big deal. We'll change it. Come on, show me how."

Hope's mouth eased shut. "I can't."

The first pang of dread sunk low in my stomach like too much food at the tone of her voice. "What do you mean?"

Her hands shook as she twisted her fingers together. "There is no spare."

I refocused on the flat. That couldn't be right. All cars had a spare.

Hope shook her head like she could read my thoughts. "That is the spare."

She had to be wrong. "The flat is the spare?"

Her wide eyes met mine. "Yes. I had a flat a week ago, and Dad helped me put the spare on. We were going to replace it, but..."

A manic laugh burst from my chest. "No. You're joking with me. I'm sure your dad would have put something in the back for you. You can't just drive around without a spare. Let's take a look."

Hope inclined her head toward me. "Ariel, I'm not joking." She tossed me her keys. "Look for yourself."

The keys fell in the dirt beside me. I grabbed them, shook the soil off, and pressed the trunk button. There was a beep and a click as the trunk popped open. With faltering steps, I made my way toward it.

There was no way this could be happening. I lifted the cover but found the compartment, where the spare should've been, completely empty.

I dropped the keys and leaned against the back of the car.

We couldn't give up. There had to be someone who could help. Besides, not everyone evacuated.

I checked the road, but it was void of cars. What were our chances of finding a spare that could work on Hope's ancient car?

We had to at least try.

"We've got to find someone who can help."

Hope caught the urgency in my voice. "You think?"

"Yes. Let's go."

I jogged toward the driveway. Hope's footfalls sounded behind me, but soon faded. I tried to look over my shoulder—but my head refused to turn.

A buzzing sounded in my ears, and everything went black.

2:00 PM

Lake house

I woke to the sensation of wet fingers on my brow. Opening my eyes, I found Hope hovering over me.

She released a gasp of relief. "Oh, thank God. I was afraid you might not wake up. How do you feel?"

I tried to sit up, but she held me down. "Wait a few minutes before you stand."

My head was propped on top of something soft. As my vision came more into focus, I discovered that Hope was sitting on the grass in front of the lake house, and my head rested on her lap. Leaves rustled in the trees above us as the water swished in the lake from the rough breezes.

Hope ran her fingers through my hair like a concerned mother. "When is the last time you ate?"

I furrowed my brows, trying to think. When *was* the last time I had eaten something?

"Ariel, this is bad," Hope said. "We need to get you something to eat.

Anna's voice materialized at the mention of food.

"Eating will only make you uglier. I'm surprised Hope wants to help you. You know Jax left you because of how fat you are, right?"

What? No. I left Jax. Right?

But my foggy brain couldn't make sense of my dazed memories.

Hope's voice cut through the static of my thoughts. "Do you have a key so we can get inside?"

My thoughts only seemed to focus when presented with a concrete question. "There's one in the back. Help me sit up."

Hope supported my back as I propped myself into a sitting position. The world spun and went black for a brief second as I regained my equilibrium. "You okay?"

"Yeah," I lied. At least my vision had cleared though. "Help me up. The key is at the back door."

Hope supported me as I found my footing, and together we hobbled toward the back door—although *I* did most of the hobbling. A headache pounded against my skull like a toddler playing with pots and a wooden spoon. Hope released me once we reached the deck, which led into the kitchen.

Crouching, I found the key hidden in a loose board on the deck, then I unlocked the house.

With the first sweep of the open door came the scent of disuse. I sneezed as I walked into the house, and the smell became stronger, like dust and stale air. Not a bad smell, but a sad one—especially since all my memories of this place were filled with life and sunshine. I knew renters had stayed a few weeks before, but the house had been locked tight since the cleaning service left at the end of the renter's stay.

Hope followed me into the kitchen and told me to sit at the barnwood kitchen table. She scoured the kitchen cupboards and pantry until she found crackers and peanut butter. After running the faucet for a few minutes, she brought a fresh glass of water to me.

Once she sat down with me, she must have noticed that I hadn't even touched a cracker yet. She dipped one into the peanut butter and placed it into her mouth. "Eat," she said.

When my hand began to shake and fear clamped its lock on

my mouth, Hope rested her elbows on the table and sighed. "I'm worried about you."

"She's trying to make you fatter," Anna said. "Don't listen to her. You don't need her as your friend. You only need me."

The smell of peanut butter reminded me of peanut butter cookies. The desire for just a taste enticed me.

"It will make you fat," Anna said.

I swallowed and centered my attention on Hope. I'd just passed out from not eating or drinking all day. My last bite of food was the banana bread I spit into the pond the day before. I'd made a promise to Hanna and Mom that I'd eat—but my fingers felt paralyzed if I attempted to bring food to my mouth.

I needed to go to treatment if I wanted to live. Listening to Anna was dangerous, but how could I turn off her voice?

Hope's shimmery black hair swept in front of her face as she leaned closer, tilting her head. "Remember when, in the seventh grade, you came to my house almost every day after school to swim with me in the pool?" She smiled at the memory. "Mom would make us Pizza Rolls, and we'd swim for hours until we could hardly pull ourselves out of the water. You'd fall asleep on the couch while we watched movies before your mom picked you up."

The memory scratched at the part of my brain that strove to keep Anna front and center. I nodded. "I remember."

"Could you do that now?" Hope asked. "Could you swim for hours?"

I forced myself to pick up a cracker. "I don't know."

She ate another peanut butter-covered cracker. "No, you couldn't." She pushed the jar of peanut butter closer. "I want the old Ariel back. The one who used to swim with me and eat Pizza Rolls. The one who could run the hallways at school and enjoy lunch with me."

Emotion clogged my throat. I could never be that girl again.

Treatment might help, sure, but it wouldn't help enough to transform me into the old Ariel. "I'm not her anymore."

A sad smile stretched across Hopes face. "But you could be."

Anna bristled. "Stop listening to her. You want me in your life and you know it."

I closed my eyes at the sound of Anna's voice, and released the cracker. It crumbled on the table. I willed myself to pick the pieces back up and eat it—to become the girl Hope had encouraged me to be. But Anna was too strong, and the cracker was too heavy between my fingers.

Years of listening to Anna's voice had dulled my logic. There is a reason that eating disorders are called a mental illness.

I left Hope and walked into the living room, out the front door, and onto the porch that overlooked the lake. A beautiful paved trail wound around the entire three miles of Lake Hollingsworth. On an average day, bikers, walkers, and joggers filled the paved pathway, but today a lone person walked in the distance.

I lowered myself onto one of the rocking chairs.

As I studied the lake, memories exploded in my mind. Images popped along the surface of my vision before I could shove them away.

Mom and Dad, sitting with me at the campfire along the shore, roasting marshmallows in the flames.

Kayaking and roller skating with Mom around the lake.

Shooting fireworks off on the Fourth of July.

Mom and Dad arguing in the kitchen about him leaving.

Lying down on the couch as we watched a movie—my head against Mom's chest as I pretended like I didn't know she was crying.

Sitting on the front porch in my bathing suit with red Popsicle juice running down my arm and a soggy stick between my fingers. Dad returning home, angry.

Mom yelling.

Me running.

Anna.

I met Anna at Lake Hollingsworth the summer I turned thirteen. I'd overheard Mom and Dad fighting in the kitchen.

"Both of us need you here. You're wasting your life working the way you do."

"Everything I do is for you. Don't you see that?"

"I don't want it. Ariel doesn't want it. We want you here. With us." Desperation leaked through Mom's words, breaking her voice. "Please stay."

"I can't."

For a moment, there was a pause. Then, "What can I do to make you change your mind?"

I heard Dad shuffling around the kitchen, opening cupboards and then slamming them shut. "Where do you hide the coffee?"

"Jeremy, what can I do to make you stay?"

Without hesitating, he said, "First of all, you can lose a few pounds. Having Ariel never sat right on your hips."

Mom was silent for a minute. When she spoke again, her voice came back strong. "How dare you! I don't regret a *thing* about Ariel. She's all I have now that you leave all the time. I'd chose her over my twenty-year-old body any day."

"I've gotta go. I'll get coffee on my way to the Orlando airport."

"Are you seeing someone else?"

Dad didn't answer.

"If you are, and if she's *prettier* than me," Mom said, using her mocking tone, "then I hope you see my face the next time you're with her. I hope you remember that the band on your finger isn't just another ring."

"If you think I'm cheating on you, then go ahead. Divorce me. You really think I'll stop you?"

Dad's nonchalant way of saying that hurt my feelings. It was as if that was how he viewed our family.

Not valuable enough, worthy enough, to fight for.

"I stay because I still love you and I have hope for us. Not just that. Ariel needs you, too, you know."

Dad's laugh was bitter. "Right. You don't stay because of me. Face the truth, honey. The only reason you haven't left yet is because of the money."

"Get out."

"Oh, so now you want me to go?" he sneered.

I couldn't take any more. I skirted across the hardwood floors on my socks and into my bedroom. I laced on my tennis shoes, then ran out the front door.

I didn't understand why Dad thought Mom needed to lose weight or why he didn't seem to like me. Mom was beautiful. And up until that moment, I'd thought I was decent-looking too. But his rant made me wonder, and I worried that maybe someday a man wouldn't like me if I gained weight, either.

Maybe I should lose a few pounds too.

And that was when I first met Anna. She appeared to me on the trail, and she told me to run. So that's what I did. Afterwords, I felt a release. I felt stronger. We became instant friends. She coached me that summer, and my mind absorbed her every word. Anna was beautiful and had her life figured out—whereas mine was falling apart. She knew how to help me.

She *was* me. Just a better version. A version that could control something in her life. Food.

The sound of Hope dragging a chair across the wood-paneled porch brought me back to the present.

I'd been to treatment once before. What made me think this time would work if last time didn't? What hope did I have of evicting Anna from my life?

A terrible, crashing thought darkened my brain. If I couldn't beat Anna, then maybe I had no choice but to simply succumb to her.

"I don't know if I can be the girl you want me to be," I said to Hope.

She looked at me with a steady gaze. "Do you mean that in your heart? I think you do want to be her again. But you're scared. Your eating disorder holds you back."

The thought of being my old self terrified me. The old Ariel wasn't as lovable as the new one. She weighed more and was less physically appealing.

"I want my best friend back," Hope said.

I swallowed but couldn't find the strength to answer.

Hope nodded once. "I'll fight with you."

"There's nothing to fight."

She reached for my hand and squeezed. "There is *every-thing* to fight."

Her determination to help me made me believe, just for a brief second, that it was possible. That it could work.

But Anna made me refuse. "I'm fighting myself, Hope. You can't help me."

That did it. Hope released her hold from my hand, stood, and walked away.

Great. I just scared off my last friend.

But moments later, she returned with the crackers and peanut butter. "I'll prove to you that I can help." She set the food in my lap.

I picked up a cracker, fighting the urge to throw it toward the lake.

Just eat it.

"Don't." Anna's remark was instant.

It's just one.

"One leads to two, which will then lead to fifty. It's impossible to eat *just one* cracker."

The image of Mom arguing with Jennifer at WHT came to

mind. Then I thought of the brownie incident at school, how I couldn't go to the coffee shop with Jax. And the banana bread and the mess I made in the pond. Finally, my fainting spell that occurred less than an hour ago.

If that was me trying to win a battle, then I was losing. Big time.

A spark of hope swelled in my chest—but it dissipated as soon as I remembered the truth. That I was too broken to be pieced back together.

I dropped the single cracker onto the porch, handed the box of crackers and jar of peanut butter to Hope, then headed inside.

3:00 PM

Lake house

Hope sat with me on the couch as we contemplated our options. She refused to leave me to find a spare tire, and we were both terrified of calling our parents. We turned on the TV and discovered that the Governor of Florida had held a press conference, pleading with people in evacuation areas to leave immediately. Irma had almost reached the Keys, and both Disney and Universal were closing their parks.

We weren't in an evacuation zone, but we were trapped.

I muted the TV. "I have to call Mom. Maybe she can get us. I'm sure she's home with Grandma by now. But if Mom can't pick us up, do you think your parents could?"

Hope shook her head. "My dad's church is being used as a shelter for the hurricane. They won't be able to get away."

"But if nobody picks us up then we're stuck here."

Her gaze remained fixed on the silent TV. "We literally have no other options."

"Fine. I'll call now."

But Mom didn't answer.

Finally, Hope gathered the courage to call her mom. "Hey, Mom." She paused to listen. "Yeah, I'm with Ariel." Pause. "Listen, I'm kind of in a situation . . ." Hope waited. "Please don't be mad—but I'm kind of stuck in Lakeland, Florida with a flat tire. I don't have another spare. Ariel tried to call her mom to get us, but she won't answer." She cringed as she held the phone to hear ear. Her mom must have been raising her voice, because even I could hear her muffled response. "I know, I know, I lied. I'm sorry. It was for a good cause. Ariel's mom got some bad news, and Ariel wanted to get the generator from the lake house to help cheer her up."

Hope squeezed her eyes shut. "Yeah, I'm sure her mom will pick us up. I'll call you when I'm on my way home. Love you too. Bye."

The TV remote in my hand suddenly felt as heavy as a ten-pound dumbbell. "Why can't she come?"

The air between us filled with trepidation. "She assumed your mom was on her way. There was a lot of noise in the background. I think people are already arriving at the church."

"She might not be able to—but I'll try calling again." I dialed her number but was met with the same result. This time I decided to leave a message. After ending the call, I looked at Hope and said, "There's nothing else we can do."

She stood. "Looks like we'll need to find a place to bunker down. Especially if we have to stay here alone for the hurricane."

We decided that the closet underneath the staircase was the best option, so we spent the next hour dusting, vacuuming, and filling the closet with blankets and pillows. Hope raided the pantry and found as much canned food as she could—even though some cans were expired—along with granola bars, crackers, pretzels, and cereal the last renters must have left behind.

By five o'clock, we were as prepared as we could be. A stash of batteries, as well as a few flashlights, sat in one corner of the closet, along with candles, bottled water, food, and some clothes we'd found.

Hope said she felt useless and needed something to do with her hands, so she went into the kitchen to make something to eat with whatever food she could find.

Mom finally called me at five past six. "Hey, Mom."

"Where are you? We just got home. Are you with Hope? You should come home now."

I turned the TV off. "I am with Hope, but . . . I can't come home."

Mom's voice raised two octaves. "Are you okay?"

My heart ached. She'd be even more worried if she knew the truth about my fainting. "I'm fine. It's just—Mom, I did something stupid." I told her about our trip to Lakeland and the flat tire. "Can you come get us?"

The quiet that followed made me wonder if we'd been disconnected. I checked the screen, but it told me that she was still on the other end. "Mom?"

A sob broke the stillness on the line. "I can't, Ariel. Is Hope with you?"

"Yes, she's in the kitchen." I held the phone closer to my ear, swallowing the lump in my throat. "Why can't you come?"

"Your grandma. She fractured her ankle, so she needs help doing everything. And if I got stuck there too . . ."

"Is there not anyone else who could watch her?"

Mom's voice was stern when she spoke again. "Listen to me, Ariel. I can't leave. I might risk it if you were alone, but Hope is with you and I trust her. She's a strong, level-headed girl, and I—I'll just have to pray that you two will be all right."

"But Mom . . . can you—?" My words came out panicked and breathless.

"Stop it, Ariel, and listen." She waited for me to calm my

breathing. "It's not just Grandma. It's the car. I'm almost out of gas."

"You can use the extra from the garage."

"We gave it to a neighbor for their generator when we got home."

"Why can't the neighbor watch Grandma while you come get us?"

"They are elderly. Now listen." I quieted. "I want you to call me every hour. You can ride out the storm in the closet under—"

"The stairs. I know. Hope and I have it stocked already, just in case."

Mom exhaled with relief. "See, I knew she was smart girl." I ignored the slight to myself. In her defense, I was very sick, so I guess trusting Hope *was* a better option than trusting me. "The rain is coming. That old house is sturdy. You'll be okay."

I could tell she was trying to be as optimistic as possible. I knew she'd come and pick me up if she could. But since Grandma couldn't go to the bathroom or get food for herself, then she needed someone with her. Plus, I did have Hope.

Still, it was hard to comprehend that I would be away from her during the storm.

"I want to be with you," I said with a soft cry.

"Shh, I know. I want you here, too, but I believe you will be okay as far as the storm is concerned." I knew what she didn't say—that the storm might not kill me.

But I could be a danger to myself.

"What about treatment?"

"We'll cross that hurdle when we come to it. Now, let me talk to Hope."

"But—"

"Now, Ariel."

I dragged my feet into the kitchen and handed the phone to Hope. I sat at the kitchen table and listened as they spoke.

Their conversation was clearly about me and how I needed to eat. Hope must have forgotten to tell Mom about my fainting—because if she had, then I think Mom would have stolen the gasoline back from the elderly neighbors, left Grandma to fend for herself, picked us up, and admitted me to the hospital.

Hope hung up and handed the phone back to me. "Go watch a movie. I'll bring food to you in a bit. I'll call my parents while the nachos cook."

Nachos? For real?

I noticed the worry that hovered over her expression. "What do you think will happen with your parents?"

"They won't be able to come. I know that'll make them furious, but I don't have any other choice."

"I'm sorry," I said, pausing in the doorway. "This is all my fault. Couldn't they send someone for us?"

Hope gave me a sad smile. "I'll ask. Go sit. I'll be out in a few minutes."

7:00 PM
Lake house

I ate a total of five corn chips, which were topped with the melted cheese and ground beef that Hope had found in the freezer. Five seemed like far too many.

I set my plate aside. "I'm going to take a shower. You can pick a movie. We might as well watch what we can before the power goes out."

She examined my almost-full plate. "You have to eat something."

"I did."

"I mean you need to eat *more*. I promised your mom I'd look out for you."

The chips were smothered in gooey cheese, beef, and salsa. Even the sight of them made my stomach cramp.

What would happen if I died here? With Hope? Would she carry that guilt with her for the rest of her life? A tug-of-war went on inside my head, which didn't exactly help my headache. "I'll try to finish eating after I take my shower."

By distancing myself from the food, I'd calm my racing heart. Or was my racing heart a sign that it was working extra hard because my body was literally about to shut down?

I locked myself in the bathroom. The house looked old on the outside, but almost every room had been refurbished to look like it came from a magazine. The downstairs bathroom in particular was modern and bright. The shower alone could have fit my whole family. The floor was made of gray-speckled tile, and the showerhead was wide as a large frying pan.

I turned the knob and peeled my clothes off, waiting for the water to steam up the interior of the bathroom.

A huge mirror was plastered onto the wall above the sink, and if I stood back, I could see myself from the thighs up. I wrapped my arms around my ribcage and studied my reflection.

Ever-present Anna pointed at a blob of skin below by cadaverous ribs. "If you could lose that, you'd be perfect."

I bent to find the scale under the sink. When was the last time I had weighed myself? I was accustomed to doing it every day, but the hurricane had interrupted my normal schedule.

I leaned over to slide the scale out—but as I straightened myself back into standing position, darkness swam into my vision. I lost control over my eyes. They had rolled into the back of my head, and my brain—it felt like it was filled with helium. My legs went limp beneath me. I could no longer carry the weight of myself.

I gripped the edge of the sink for support, keeping myself from falling. But the muscles in my arms had deadened and were immobilized.

My knees hit the cold tile as I fell. My heart beat hard in my chest as I gasped for breath, remaining in a crawling position.

After a few seconds, my eyes returned to normal, restoring my vision. The strength and feeling of my limbs seemed to have returned to normal too.

I set my forehead on the scale. If Hope would have walked in, she might have thought I worshiped it. In a sense, maybe I did.

Tears blurred my vision. It felt like there were fists in my chest kneading bread dough because of my rapid pulse.

Fainting twice in one day could not be good. My throat and head throbbed. The arms that attempted to hold me upright shook. Panic gripped me. *Could I be having a heart attack? Or worse—am I dying?*

Taking advantage of the meager amount of feeling in my limbs, I pushed myself off the floor and draped my upper half over the sink to turn on the cold water. I sucked it down, trying to fill my stomach and feed my body.

Some of the dizziness subsided. My heartbeat began to slow and fall back into its normal rhythm.

Steam covered the mirror, and thick fog obscured the bathroom.

I stumbled into the shower, allowing the water to wash over my naked body. A body I was beginning to fear.

Anna watched me from the other side of the glass. "Don't stop now, Ariel. You'll look like me soon enough."

I wanted to believe her. But she had said the same thing for years. I was starting to believe that maybe that day would never arrive.

At least, not without me destroying myself in the process.

8:00 PM
Lake house

After my shower, I used my newfound fear of self-destruction to polish off the plate of nachos. I knew that my fainting was probably a result of my internal organs shutting down and then sparking back to life. Food was the only thing that could help to keep them alive.

After a movie, my stomach stretched with food and eyelids drooped with fatigue. "I'm going to bed."

Hope turned off the TV. "I'll come too."

We called my mom, and with her direction she agreed that sleeping in one of the downstairs bedrooms would be safe for one more night. Hope dragged a mattress into the room and insisted that I sleep in the bed.

It only took a few minutes for me to fall asleep, but I can still remember the last thought that tortured my mind in those final seconds.

Will I wake up tomorrow? And if I do, what will happen when the hurricane hits?

Chapter 13

Present
            March 6th, 2018

KELLY SHUTS the journal and hands it back to me. "What emotions did you experience as you wrote about fainting in the bathroom?"

You know that half-swallow you do in the back of your throat when you try not to cry? That happens when she asks. A yearning and sadness wash over me in equal measures, but they are overshadowed by the dark EMOTION that fills me. I don't know how else to describe it. It's not grief, joy, anger, jealously, greed, or happiness. It's all of them and none of them at the same time. I can only describe it as big, heavy, and oppressing.

It is memory.

I don't answer her because I can't. In typical counselor fashion, she presses harder by asking the same question in different words. Cue the cliché eye roll.

"How did you feel when you wrote about fainting in the bathroom and seeing Anna standing over you?"

Anna's name on her tongue transforms my wad of emotion into tears. "When I wrote about her . . . I wanted her back just as much as I wanted to kill her again."

Kelly nods like she understands, but how could she? "You've made progress, and inviting Anna back into your life could erase all you've accomplished."

"But I miss her." I hate to admit it, but I do. The same way a toddler misses the habit of having a pacifier to comfort them, I miss Anna. She was my comfort.

"Who is Anna to you, Ariel?"

"A friend."

Kelly crossed her legs. "Is she the kind of friend you want to have? In what ways did she brighten your life? What benefits did you receive from the friendship?"

I think about this. It's a trick question, because of course eating disorders don't have real-world benefits. They have personal temporary ones. Hope is a good friend who stayed with me when things were hard. Jax—whom I've been spending more time with—encourages me. Anna . . . well, in a way, she completes me. She doesn't have a benefit. To be honest, her grip has been slipping—and that scares me. Ever since I ate that small bag of Doritos at the gas station, I've noticed her fade to the background. This frightens me, because living without her seems wrong after almost four years.

Kelly waits for an answer, but I don't have any.

My body and mind are in a war with each other. Like the too-small blue bra and the bigger black bra, I am having trouble finding my place in life. Finding my place in recovery. Who am I if I don't have Anna? What does life look like without her, and is it even possible? My desire ping-pongs between the blanket of comfort she offers me and the freedom I've experienced without her—the health, healed relationships, and new life.

Kelly changes tact, clearly satisfied that she's caused me to think. "What will you write next?"

I run my hands over the journal in my lap, which is filled with words and waiting to be filled with more. "The hurricane."

"What significant event happened that day in regard to your eating disorder?"

I look past Kelly and toward the sea green wall with abstract blue and white paintings. "It's the day I killed her."

"Then what happened?"

I meet her eyes again. "I ended up here."

"How?"

My fingers twitch to write. I've almost reached the end of Anna. What I'm communicating with now is her ghost. I haven't fully resurrected her yet. I've taken Kelly's advice to heart and am waiting until I write the end—and now, I am here.

Chapter 14

S*unday, September 10th, 2017*

10:00 AM

Lake house

A sound like a million sprinkles hitting the tile floor of the kitchen woke me. The slow expanding and deflating of Hope's ribcage as she lay against a mattress on the floor brought my attention to her form. The room was as dark as if the sun were about to rise. I checked my phone. It was almost ten o'clock. The day was dark, and the sound that had awoken me was the rain tapping against the window.

I tiptoed from bed and drew the curtain aside an inch. Water streaked the glass as droplets splattered the panes.

Hurricane Irma was near.

Hope stirred and groaned. "What time is it?"

"Ten."

"Really?" She reached for her phone and spent a few moments clicking, and then said, "Ariel, this isn't good. They really think the hurricane will hit the Gulf Coast. This article says the storm surge could wipe away whole houses. Towns like Tampa could be decimated. We're closer to the Gulf Coast than the Atlantic." She squirmed and looked out the window. "We shouldn't be anywhere near the eye of the storm, but things could still get bad. They say the right side of the storm is the strongest—and that's exactly where we are."

"I'll call my mom. But it's already started . . . and I'm afraid there's nothing we can do."

12:00 PM

Lake house

Hope and I tracked Irma's progress as she overtook the Florida Keys and swayed in our direction. We sat on the couch with the TV turned off and watched the wind blow rain sideways from the front porch windows. We knew it wouldn't be safe to continue sitting there if the winds grew stronger, but at the moment, we were content to have a front row seat. We'd take refuge below the staircase when the storm passed overhead. But would it be enough to keep us safe?

When we grew bored of watching the rain fall sideways, Hope found cans of soup in the kitchen and heated them on the stove.

I couldn't eat, but Hope still made me sit at the kitchen table with her.

"Eat," she said.

I calculated the calories in the broth, noodles, vegetables, and chicken. The fact that my brain did this bothered me, because my heart beat almost painfully in my chest, as if it struggled to keep its rhythm. Instead of telling Hope, I forced myself to take a spoonful of broth that contained a chunk of carrot. Bringing the spoon to my mouth was like deadlifting hundreds of pounds on the end of a kitchen utensil. I summoned Anna.

This is crazy. Why won't you let me eat?

"Why are you asking me such a stupid question, fatty?"

Seriously, I'm going to die.

"At least you won't be fat."

Is that worth dying for?

"You'll be fine. You've perused enough *thinspo* websites to know there are girls way skinnier than you. You're a whale compared to them. If even they are still alive, then you will definitely be all right. Treatment is just around the corner. There are only a few days left to keep yourself in line."

My thoughts were interrupted by a branch that pinged against the window. Soup splashed from my spoon as I jerked in my seat.

Great, now I had to force the soup back to my mouth again.

"Talk to me," I said to Hope. Talking was better than being overtaken by the darkness of my thoughts.

Her bowl of soup was already half empty. "About what?"

Desperation gathered in my soul. "Anything."

She understood my cue and engaged me in conversation while I forced myself to eat half of my bowl of soup. But if I were to be honest with myself, I could only eat the broth and vegetables. The chicken and noodles were left behind.

2:00 PM

Lake house

Something expanded in my chest throughout the day as Hope and I alternated between watching movies and watching the building storm. Restlessness made my muscles jump, and my thoughts scattered around topics but always landed back on Anna. She was all I could think about.

Eventually exhaustion took over my body—weariness from the fight and impending storm. So I took a nap.

5:00 PM
Lake house

After my nap, Hope and I watched two movies. An inner premonition suggested something bad was approaching, but I shrugged it off and blamed the hurricane rather than my own emotional turmoil. The power still hadn't gone out, so I wondered if the storm would really get as bad as they had predicted. Rain still pelted against the windows, and the wind sashayed branches across the sky—but nothing other than leaves were swirling with the rain and wind. It wasn't like the tornado winds in *The Wizard of Oz*. Not yet, at least.

Hope gasped beside me. "Turn on the news."

I switched from *Guardians of the Galaxy Vol. 2* to a local station.

The camera angle showed the walking trail built against downtown Tampa Bay, but there was no bay. The water that should have filled Tampa Bay, was gone. In its place was exposed sand. People clambered over the rail and into the bay to take photos and walk in a place that was normally filled with water.

"Idiots," Hope murmured, but then she shrugged. "It does look fun though. I'd do it."

"Where did the water go?"

The newswoman wore a raincoat with its hood up as rain sprayed over her. "Irma's winds are responsible for this phenomenon. If you look behind me, you will see that parts of Tampa Bay have been emptied and—"

"How could a hurricane empty Tampa Bay? It's huge."

Hope chewed her bottom lip. "I don't know, but can you

imagine what that's going to look like when the water rushes back in? It'll hit downtown like a tidal wave."

The image on the screen switched to palm trees bending in strong winds, and cars submerged as water ran through the streets of Miami.

The eye of the storm would arrive in a few hours. There was no doubt that Irma was large enough to engulf the entire state of Florida.

The sheets of rain we saw out the front window were only the bands surrounding her eye. It would only get worse from there.

9:30 PM

Lake house

Wind howled against the house as it searched, with its strong gusts, for cracks in the siding. Hope and I had turned off all the lights. We huddled in the kitchen, watching the trees bend in the gale. Every so often we'd hear a click against the roof where I'd assumed shingles were scrapped off like unwanted pepperonis on a slice of pizza. Small limbs clicked against the window in the kitchen as they were snapped from their branches and hurtled through the storm.

We watched all of this with fear and awe. We should have been in the closet, but we couldn't stop watching yet.

The darkness outside triggered the darkness within myself. An obsessive compulsive-like urge took over me, and I stumbled toward the bathroom, the crescendo in my head as loud as the wind outside.

"Where are you going?" Hope asked.

"To the bathroom." She didn't ask any more questions, but I sensed that she followed me.

Light almost blinded me as I snapped on the switch. I

slammed the bathroom door, cutting off Hope's path. How could the power still be on? I counted the light as a blessing and waited for my eyes to adjust to the glare of the bathroom. When they did, I confronted Anna in the glass. "I don't want to die."

Anna—the girl I wanted to be—tantalized me with the image of myself that I strove to become. "What do you want, then?"

"I want to be beautiful, but I want to live too."

"I want you to die."

The words struck me, because she'd never said anything like that before. She'd always encouraged me to be stronger, to have more self-control. But my self-control was killing me. Literally. *Anna* was killing me. The realization morphed Anna from the beautiful girl I wanted to become into a monster as I realized her true intentions.

But we'd been together so long. I couldn't let her go. I wanted her in my life. Not just that—I needed her. "Why would you want me to die?" Maybe I had misunderstood her.

"Either you choose me and get the perfect body you've always wanted, or you choose to listen to the counselors at WHT who will make you fat. Your choice."

"But if I keep listening to you, then I might die."

Anna shrugged. "Maybe. Maybe not. You'll never know unless you try."

"I'm afraid of dying."

"The things worth fighting for are hard to attain. There's always some risk involved."

"Risking my life isn't worthwhile. My life isn't a business deal."

Realizing she didn't have the same hold on me as she did before, she morphed back into the beautiful girl—but it was too late. I'd seen her for what she truly was. "If you let go of me, then you'll never have the same control over your life as you do now. You love the way controlling your weight by the food you eat and the way you exercise make you feel."

She was right. I did. But was it worth my life? I thought of my mom and the summers we'd enjoyed at this very house. I thought of Hope, Jax, and Tara. If I allowed Anna to keep controlling me, then I might not have a chance to live, and I'd never have a chance to know if I could have conquered my demons.

"I can't do this anymore." I told Anna.

"Can't do what?"

"Continue listening to you."

She scoffed. "So, what are you going to do? *Kill me?* You can't get rid of me. We are the same person. Ariel is Anna, and Anna is Ariel."

That was the moment I knew I had to kill the part of myself I loved the most; that way, I could discover parts of my life that I didn't yet know. I couldn't pursue life while Anna blocked my view. I wasn't completely sure what I wanted out of life, but I needed the chance to at least find out.

I opened the cabinet, searching for something heavy.

"What are you doing?" Anna demanded.

I'm crying as I write this. I remember the cold tile of the floor and the raw determination I had to find something I could use to smash the glass. The same type of compulsion that halts me from eating now wanted to get rid of the thing that was trying to kill me then. The problem was—the thing killing me was a part of myself. Severing Anna from me was like killing a best friend, a sister, a twin.

I ignored her. If I didn't follow through with it, then I knew I might not have the courage later.

I found the scale under the sink. Anna's image blurred as the scale shook in my hands.

"Don't do this," she said. "You're my best friend."

The scale was old and had a needle that swung like a

pendulum. I coughed on a sob as I lifted it like a baseball bat, the needle winking with the movement. "You're my best friend too."

Anna cried as hard as I did. "I love you."

The scale slipped against my sweaty fingers. I lowered it a few inches.

This was stupid. I couldn't kill her. She was right—it wasn't that easy. I didn't want her to die. But if I'd let her kill me, then I'd never know the kind of life I could've had.

That was my motivation: I wanted to discover who I could become.

I opened my mouth and screamed louder and longer than ever before. I could only see Anna's silhouette through my blurry eyes. "I love you too," I said—then I lifted the scale and swung it toward the mirror. Anna shattered into hundreds of sharp pieces. Shards fell from the wall, skittered across the counter, and tinkled across the floor.

I fell to my knees in the glass, sharp edges cutting into my knees. The scale fell from my fingers and broke against the tile.

Weary, my vision blurred, and I set my hands against the glass-covered floor to keep from falling face first into the sharp fragments.

Hope stepped into the bathroom, finding me on the floor surrounded by broken glass. Blood seeped from cuts on my hands and knees. Glass crunched under her feet as she stooped to help me up. When did she put on shoes? I leaned my weight against her, allowing her to lead me from the room.

"What happened?"

"I don't want to die," I said in a flat voice. I didn't feel the pain of the cuts.

"Okay," she said. "But what does that have to do with the broken mirror?"

"I killed her."

Hope didn't ask me what I meant. She knew. She hugged me tight.

A monstrous crack came from outside, followed by what sounded like pots, pans, and silverware falling from the sky and crashing. Hope grabbed my hand and pulled me toward the stairs. She shoved me into the closet and slammed the door behind us.

My jaw shook as I tried to keep the fear from shaking my whole body. "What was that?"

Her hand grabbed mine in the dark. "I think a tree just fell."

We huddled together beneath the staircase. Hope wrapped my bleeding hands in a towel. Crashes and bangs, along with the sound of shingles ripping away from the roof, caused my mind to envision multiple scenarios in which we died. I kept anticipating the sound of a loud snap, and then the crushing weight of a tree—or even the house itself—falling on top of us.

Anna was dead. But that didn't mean my life wasn't still in danger.

Chapter 15

Present
March 17th, 2018

I sit in the front seat of Mom's Toyota Highlander, tension knotting my neck enough to cause a slight headache. The man who tests my driving sits in the passenger seat, a clipboard across his knees. *I can do this*, I remind myself. *Mom said I'm ready.*

The radio is off, and the sound of air humming past the car is the only noise in this anxiety filled vehicle. Well, the anxiety is on my part. The test administrator is a thirty-something-year-old guy who keeps checking his phone. I open my mouth to tell him I'm just as eager to be done with this test as he is, but I think better of it. He might mark off points for my snarky attitude.

As we drive along the highway, he points and says, "Take this exit."

My turn signal clicks as I flip it on and merge into the exit lane. The road ahead continues straight—but to my dismay, the man points left. "Turn here."

I knew I'd need to make a left turn. But now that it's actually here, my muscles tense and my brain goes wild with worry. I tap the brake as the solid red light turns to a green arrow.

I suck in a quick breath of surprise. I won't have to question myself on this one, because the green arrow does all my hard work for me. I want to do a fist pump but refrain myself. I also think this movement will lose me points with this man—although apparently he is *still* checking his phone.

As I turn my attention away from the man to finish the left turn, a silver SUV speeds through the red light—and my foot can't reach the brake pedal fast enough.

A flash of silver. Then . . .

Crash!

Inky darkness swirls in my vision. Are we tilting? Rolling? I can't tell. The sound of metal on metal and glass crunching and crashing is too loud. My neck whips back and forth like a crazy roller coaster ride, causing my brain to pound against my skull.

Did the man beside me yell? I think so, but I'm not sure. We were hit on his side, right? Panic seizes my heart. Is he okay?

My sense of direction becomes lost. First, I'm upside down. Then on my side. Then right-side up. Then on my side again.

We must be rolling. What if we roll into more traffic and get hit again? Am I about to die?

My thoughts move faster than our smashed car—yet the dull buzz in my head makes it feel like my thoughts swim in slow motion.

Then the rolling comes to a sudden halt. I peel my eyes open—when did I close them?—and notice that I lie against the door, the driver's side pressed against what looks like asphalt and a solid yellow line.

Looking up, I let out a scream. The man hangs from his seat belt above me. My head throbs, and I'm not sure how to move my arms—or if I even should. It doesn't seem like a good idea to lift my head, so I keep it relaxed against the road instead. Glass bites the skin of my temple.

A loud beeping slices through my frazzled brain. Is that coming from my car or another?

Frantic speech. Shoes crunching glass. The murmur of voices, calling out to me, asking questions—if I'm okay. If I can move. If anything is broken.

But I can't seem to formulate a response.

My vision blurs—or maybe my eyes are shutting. I force my eyelids apart, staring at the hanging man. Is he dead?

My eyelids—they're too heavy.

A final thought swims through my murky mind before I allow myself to fade.

Does this mean I failed the test?

Chapter 16

M onday, September 11th, 2017

2:00 AM
   Lake house
   I remember glancing at my phone when the wind started to die down. Hope and I had relaxed a little, and then we fell into worried sleep.

8:00 AM
   Lake house
   Hope and I woke around eight in the morning. Muted daylight filtered from underneath the door—not sunshine, but a clouded light. Hope turned the knob and pushed the door open.
   Our first view outside of our haven was the hallway wall. Nothing extraordinary. Better than seeing that the house had crashed around us.

We ducked under the doorframe and stood in the empty hallway. Hope tried a switch, but nothing happened. I don't think either of us expected for there to be electricity, but we had to at least try.

We walked to the front room, pulled the blinds back, and observed what was left of our world.

The scene before us wasn't as bad as I had expected, but it was still a sight to behold. Sky the color of dark gravy cast a sinister tone against the trees that were broken in half. Branches and twigs littered the ground as if the earth had decided it wanted a new form of carpet. The road was impassible because of the fallen trees and branches. The lake had filled so high it almost pooled over the road. Cardboard, which once covered windows instead of shutters, was strewn across the ground. Irma must have laughed when she saw such minimal preparations. I was glad she hadn't blown out the windows on our house.

I sagged against the wall with fatigue. Hope wrapped her arm around my middle to support me. "You okay?"

Honesty spit out of my mouth before I could summon the compulsion to lie. "No. My chest hurts, and I'm tired."

Hope lifted me as if I were a toddler and brought me into the living room. She set me on the couch and pulled a blanket over me. "I'll get something from the stash under the stairs," she said. "One second."

When she returned, she offered me a dark chocolate peanut butter granola bar—two of my favorite things.

My brain automatically calculated the calories, but I was beyond caring. Well, I cared, but I cared about living more.

I took a bite. The bar tasted like summer days, childhood, and freedom. The nourishment fed my soul as I allowed myself to eat without guilt. I could do this. I *must* do this. If I didn't, I would die.

I swallowed. I couldn't do this.

No, I could.

I argued with *myself*, not Anna. I strove to push that distorted lens away from my perspective and instead focus on what I needed in order to stay alive. And at that second, I needed to finish the granola bar.

Hope sat on the couch beside me and dialed numbers into her cell phone. "Please work," she whispered, holding the phone up to her ear. "Yes," she said when there was a ring.

She sat close enough that I could hear when my mom answered. "Hope? Are you two okay? How is Ariel?"

"We're okay, but we can't get out. I see trees on the roads. Who knows how many more are blocking us between here and home. What should we do?"

The scent and taste of peanut butter were like water after a drought. My teeth dug through the bar as I crunched on the chunks of dark chocolate. When was the last time I had eaten like this—to feed my body, and not to punish or reward myself?

Mom's voice came from Hope's phone. "How's Ariel?"

Hope grimaced. "Not great. I think she needs to go to the hospital."

My stomach dropped at her last word. I was supposed to go to treatment, not to the hospital.

"I'll call Whole Healing Treatment today and see when they can get her in," Mom said. "Based on the looks of things here, it'll probably be a few days."

"What should I do?" Hope asked.

There was a pause for a moment before Mom responded. "Be honest, Hope. How bad is she?"

"Bad."

Apparently she wasn't afraid of admitting this truth in front of me. I wanted to punch her in the shoulder for talking about me as if I weren't beside her, but I didn't have the energy to focus on anything but eating.

"Call 911," Mom said.

"But they won't be able to—"

"Just call and see what happens."

"Are you sure?"

"I should have brought her in when Whole Healing Treatment suggested it. I want her to be safe. Will she go willingly?"

Hope faced me and raised a brow.

I forced myself to nod once.

"Yes, she'll go."

"Good. Give them a call, and then call me again to give me an update. Tell them everything."

"Okay. I'll get back with you."

"Hope?"

"Yeah?"

"Give Ariel a hug for me and tell her that I love her. I'm frustrated that you girls did what you did, but we'll deal with that later. For now, just let her know that I love her."

Hope's gaze met mine. I could tell, from her expression, that she knew I could hear.

After they said goodbye, Hope took a steadying breath. "This is for your own good," she said.

I could only watch as Hope pressed the numbers into her phone. *911.*

Chapter 17

P*resent*
March 17th, 2018

THE FIRST THING I'm conscious of is the smell of hospital anti-septic. I recognize it for its pungency. It's familiar, too, because I remember hating it when I was in the hospital last September before entering WHT. The sound of shoes squeaking on linoleum floors make me cringe—but the cringe causes pain to shoot through my left cheek. I try to lift my right hand to my face, but it's bandaged and heavy. I blink and try to focus on white ceiling tiles. The room is muted. The curtains are drawn, and the only light comes from the hallway door. I lift my neck and notice a cast on my right arm that reaches from my elbow to my fingers. An IV is attached to the back of my left hand.

With slow, careful movements, I lift my hand to my cheek and feel a bandage from my temple to jaw. So that's why cringing hurt.

The sound of shuffling draws my attention to a figure sitting on a chair beside my bed. I didn't notice it in my first scan of the room.

Mom.

She leans forward. "You're awake. How do you feel?"

I know exactly why I am here. I ask the first question that pops into my mind. "Did I pass the test?"

Mom lets out a soft laugh. She runs her fingers up and down my arm. "You didn't finish the test, honey. You finished off my car, but not the test."

"Is he dead?"

"No. He suffered a concussion and will be released later today."

"Good." I release a sigh of relief. "I thought I killed him."

"Witnesses agree that you did nothing wrong. The driver who hit you was texting." She inches her chair closer to the hospital bed and takes my entombed hand as I relax my head against the pillow and rest my eyes. "There's something we need to talk about, Ariel."

"Hmm?" I hum without opening my eyes.

"Kelly is coming."

My eyes flash open. "What? Why? This has nothing to do with her." I'm flattered but confused at the same time. Why would my counselor come to the hospital to see me after a car accident? I'm in *physical* turmoil, not emotional turmoil.

"The doctors were concerned about your vitals."

I wince as I try to contort my face into a cynical smile, but I have to settle for a grimace instead. "I got in a car accident and probably bled a lot from my face." I touch the bandage on my cheek. "Of course my vitals were off. Duh."

Mom shakes her head. "No, sweetie, it's more than that. Your BMI is low, and with your history . . ."

She doesn't have to finish. The doctors think I'm relapsing.

Am I?

I'm not sure, but I think I'm approaching the line. Anna's

voice has grown louder since I wrote about her death. You'd think the stronghold she had on me would become looser considering all I went through.

Now that I'm healthy—sans the car accident, at least—I must decide if recovery is worth it. I know it is, but sometimes it's hard to see the full picture when Anna's voice is in my brain and my old habits seem more comfortable than following meal plans. I keep thinking that skipping one meal or one snack won't hurt—but then it turns into two or three. I supplement occasionally by sometimes letting myself eat fear foods, such as Doritos or chocolate glazed donuts, but I know I'm not following all of the recovery guidelines. Now that I'm past the point of death, I need a reason to continue.

"Hope is coming, too," Mom says.

Two visitors when all I want to do is sleep? I groan.

"I'm sure they won't stay long."

I rest my head back and stare at the ceiling. "When do I get out of here?"

"I'm not sure yet. They want to keep you overnight so they can monitor your progress. You also suffered a concussion, and with your low BMI they want to make sure everything is okay."

"When will Kelly be here?"

"In an hour."

My eyes drift shut.

I ASK Mom to open the curtains to reveal the setting sun before Kelly arrives. I try to plan what I'm going to say to her and watch as the night and day mesh with each other, resulting in an orange and pink skyline that blends with the dark navy of the night. Soft footsteps draw my attention to the door.

Kelly steps inside. She wears jeans and a loose black T-shirt instead of one of the colorful blouses that she usually wears during our sessions. Her hair is up in a ponytail, and her typical ballet flats have been replaced with sneakers. "Hi, Ariel," she says.

Mom says hello, then she excuses herself from the room with the lame excuse that she's going to the bathroom in the hallway—even though my room has a perfectly good and private restroom. Kelly settles into the chair beside my bed. "How are you?"

I shrug the shoulder of my good arm. "I'm alive."

"Thank God for that." She grins at my dry humor. "So your mom asked me to come. She said the doctors were concerned."

"I heard." It's weird talking to her outside of her office, especially since she looks so . . . normal. "They don't need to be concerned though."

"Shouldn't they?"

"No. I haven't been listening to Anna that much."

"Why do you still refer to her as Anna rather than an eating disorder?"

I shift in the bed. "I prefer not to have it labeled as a diagnosis."

"Ariel, you like when I tell it how it is, right? Or do you prefer me to sugarcoat things?"

I shrug. "I prefer low sugar snacks as a rule."

Kelly smirks. Not a mean or condescending expression, but a genuine act of humor. "I'm not going to tiptoe around your eating disorder or what you've experienced. You're a smart girl. I know you are fully aware that eating disorders are mental illnesses. I do not consider you to be a diagnosis. Anorexia is a medical term that refers to a very real struggle you've faced. It's not a label."

I don't see it the same way she does. I'm seventeen years old, and being diagnosed with anorexia is most certainly a label in the same way that *slut, druggie,* or *alcoholic* is a label. When I refer to my eating disorder as Anna, it gives her life. But if we're being technical, then I guess I could be labeled as schiz-ophrenic when I name my eating disorder. But I'd rather not be associated with either term, and I am certainly not crazy.

I started thinking of my eating disorder as Anna after my first stint in treatment. Some of the other girls called their disorders *Ed*, which is short for eating disorder. That sounded creepy. Other girls called them Ana, short for anorexia. I liked that better, but I think and write about her with an extra *N*. The spelling of *Anna* looks nicer than *Ana*. It's not as harsh, in my opinion.

Kelly tries rewording her question. "Are you actively strug-gling with your eating disorder, or are you making healthy choices?"

I don't like where this is going. I don't know how to answer. "No. I haven't been struggling the same way since I killed her." Again, I have never suffered from delusions. Ask any girl who's had an eating disorder and she can probably tell you how it's like a second part of you goes crazy—like you can't control your desires or thoughts.

The counselor in Kelly makes an appearance as she crosses one leg over the other, resting her hands atop her thighs. "Eating disorders can take years—sometimes a lifetime—to overcome. It's a journey."

I'm not stupid. Everything she's telling me is what I learned in treatment and what we've discussed in counseling. I already know that recovery takes a long time. I know I have to be dedi-cated to my health.

But therein lies the issue. I'm just not sure how dedicated I actually am.

Eating disorders are like addictions. When someone has an addiction to something, such as alcohol or drugs, they abstain from them in order to recover. But you can't escape food. Instead of removing yourself from the temptation entirely, you instead have to face it. Every. Single. Day.

Multiple times a day, actually. And you must learn how to develop a good relationship with food instead of eradicating it from your life.

But, like drugs, there is a certain "high" or comfort you receive from remaining in the harmful habits. You know it's bad for you, but you can't seem to help yourself.

Think of people who smoke. Smoking literally kills you, but that fact isn't enough to keep people from doing it. Why? Because it's comfortable.

Likewise, having the company of Anna in my life is comfortable. It's like choosing between a mattress that's infested with bed bugs verses a fresh bed of pine needles. That's how both recovery and Anna are to me. Of course, the mattress is more comfortable initially, but would you rather sleep on a mattress and wake with itchy welts, or sleep on a prickly bed made of needles and wake with the fresh scent of pine?

The more I think of the pros and cons, the more I lean toward recovery. But how in the world do I follow through with it? Like quitting a drug, having a healthy relationship with food seems to be a nearly impossible feat.

Voices in the hallway keep me from voicing my thoughts to Kelly. Hope walks in, followed by—I can't see her in the dim light. But as they approach my bed, I recognize the face.

Tara.

My heart soars at the number of people who want to see me while my mind simultaneously thinks, *how many more people can we fit in this room?*

Kelly's face lights up at the sight of them. She stands from her chair, and to my surprise, gives Tara a hug.

When Hope looks at me, I mouth, "How do they know each other?"

She raises her brows and shrugs.

Tara and Kelly break from the delight of seeing each other,

then turn to me. I wait for someone to explain. Tara speaks first. "Kelly is my counselor."

What the?

Kelly comes to my side and leans down to give me a hug. "We'll talk later."

She's leaving? Why? We've hardly talked.

"Tara and I have known each other for a long time," she says. "I think the two of you should talk."

"But I—"

"Just talk," she says. "I need to get home, but I wanted to see you. We'll discuss more on Tuesday. For now, rest and think about what we discussed. You know all the right answers, but now you just have to make the decision."

"What?" I say as Kelly leaves the room.

Hope darts her gaze between the door and Tara with the same shocked expression that I probably wear as well. She gestures toward the hallway. "Who was that?"

"Kelly," I say.

"Your counselor?" She looks at Tara. "And your counselor too?"

"Yes," Tara says. "Small world."

Hope sits next to me on the bed. "Why did she leave so fast?"

Tara glances at the now-empty doorway. "Kelly and I have known each other for years. She's more than a counselor now. She's my friend. We get coffee sometimes. If she left, then she must think you're in good shape."

I keep a neutral expression to avoid the pain that contorting my face would make. "If I were in good shape, then she wouldn't have made a personal visit to my hospital room."

Tara slips her shoes off and pulls both her feet onto the end of the bed to cross her legs. I've seen her on and off since treatment. Mostly with Hope. She's encouraged me, but I've felt almost like a hypocrite for talking to her. She's got this recovery thing figured out, while I'm walking on a razor-thin line and in danger of being injured.

I open my mouth to ask her a question, but then I think better of it.

"What?" she says.

"I don't want to ask you anything too personal." Anna's voice is a personal thing, and I don't want to upset Tara, especially if she's in a good place.

"You can ask me anything. Seriously, girl." She holds her arms out. "I've got nothing to hide."

I lean forward, my elbows resting on one of the pillows that prop me up. "How are you doing, really? Do you still hear that voice in your head that tells you not to eat?"

She doesn't miss a beat. "Oh my word, yes."

My eyebrows lift in surprise. How could Kelly think Tara's a good person to talk to when she's still faced with the temptation to avoid eating?

"You do?" I ask. "But I thought you were better."

"I am," she says quickly. "I mean, I'm working on it. It's a process. I'm not sick, but I still consider myself to be in recovery. I talk to Kelly when I'm having a rough time."

The mutual connection we have with Kelly gives me a deeper sense of comfort around Tara. "Is Kelly the one who helped you decide to stick with recovery? I'm struggling, to be honest. I don't like my body. I want the control back."

The way Tara doesn't remove her gaze from mine tells me that she truly hears me. She understands. "You can't have both. But trust me—you don't want the eating disorder. It's not worth it. It's a liar."

Her decisive response leaves me momentarily speechless.

"I don't know how you feel about God," she continues. "Yes, Kelly has helped me, but 90 percent of my recovery has been rooted in my faith. Biblical promises that assure me that I'm perfect just the way I am, at whatever size, because God created me. It's my honest-to-goodness truth, despite how cheesy it might sound."

I stay quiet, but only because I'm interested. Hope watches us but doesn't speak. Did she have a hunch that Tara and I needed to talk, and that's why she brought her?

Tara and Hope aren't the polished, refined Christians that I've grown up knowing. They make mistakes, and apparently they aren't afraid to show them. They don't pretend to be perfect or tell people what they should or shouldn't do. They love through their actions, and actions mean a whole lot more than words.

"What if you were created by the God of the universe?" Tara asks. "Just think about it. If you believe that, then would you live your life any differently?"

My chest aches at the idea. I long to believe that I am worth that much thought—but I just don't think I am. I've lived so long believing the opposite. That I'm *not* good enough. How could it be possible to reframe my mindset? How could I live in a way that aligns with that belief instead?

"Believing in true beauty is the very thing that has helped me to ditch the eating disorder," she says. "I can't, in good conscious, believe I was created and am loved—while at the same time continue to listen to the voice that tells me the exact opposite. The voice that convinces me to starve myself."

I'm not afraid to be vulnerable with Tara and Hope. Both of them have seen the worst of me. "I'm not sure I believe that."

"How about this, then." She leans forward, looking me straight in the eyes, as if she were attempting to speak to my soul and not just my mind. "How would you feel if I told you that *I* think you are beautiful and that you have something to offer the world? Because I do. I think you do have something special, Ariel."

Shadows have fallen across the room. Only a sliver of the

setting sun filters through the windows and casts light on Tara's expression.

"You don't know me, though, so how could you say that?"

"Because I believe that everyone has a purpose."

"Then what makes me so special?" The words spill from my heart. It's what I've wondered for years, but I've never spoken the thought aloud. *What makes me special?*

"*You* make *you* special." Her words, and the gentle tone of her voice, illuminate the darkness. "There will never be another girl like you. Ever. Not in the past, not now, and not in the future. You can change the world because you are the only Ariel in the world. Changing the world looks different for different people. Being yourself and making your unique impact might simply involve hugging a friend or being a good daughter. Someday it might involve being a good wife or mother."

I give a nervous laugh. "Is that what Kelly taught you? I don't have many skills or hobbies. Nothing."

She shrugs. "Anything you choose to do has the potential to change the world."

"I don't think I'm a change-the-world type of girl."

"How about your own world? You wanted to know how I beat the voices. Well, Ariel, I beat them by believing that I was created. And if I was created, then I am beautiful, because artists don't create ugly art. They believe their artwork is beautiful and significant."

Hope leans her head against my shoulder.

"Whenever I have the urge to restrict food or fall into an old behavior," Tara continues, "I remember that I have a purpose, one that only I have the ability to fulfill. Even if that purpose is simply washing the sheets for my husband and I that day. It's still a purpose, big or small, and it's mine and mine alone. *That's* what makes me special. That's what motivates me to stick with health over harm."

I want to believe that what she says is true. I want to believe that I have something unique to offer the people in my life, something that only I can achieve. "I'd like that. But how do you know what your purpose is from day to day?"

She glances down for a moment, as if she's trying to think of the perfect response. Then she looks back up at me and says, "I can't answer that for you. I think, deep down, you know what you must accomplish today. Our purpose is placed on the inside of us. Others can't tell us what to do. They can direct us and help us to see our own potential, sure—but ultimately, we are the ones who are responsible in choosing how we will live and what we will believe. Does that answer your question?"

I'm not sure, so I don't respond. Tara's faith is large, expansive, and deep. She's chosen recovery because she believes in something bigger than herself. She believes she has a reason to be alive. I must have a reason, too—especially since I'm still here after already beating the odds.

But Tara's purpose seems too vast. Sure, I get that she wants to be who she was created to be—but I don't need to plan out my whole life. I just want to know what the next step is for me right now.

Why should I recover now? Why should I not refuse to eat in this moment?

A thought comes to mind. I look back at Tara and ask, "What did your purpose lead you to do today?"

When she speaks, the sincerity in her voice almost makes me want to cry.

"Reaching *today* involved taking a lot of small steps. But today, Ariel . . ." She glances at Hope, who is beside me, then looks back at me. "Today, my faith, my purpose, has brought me to you. You are my purpose for today."

Mom turns on the light when she comes back in the room. Hope, Tara, and I have spent the past 30 minutes talking and laughing in the dark. Hearing Tara talk about her recovery has given me hope that maybe I can recover too.

The reason I'm lying in a hospital bed is because I could have died today. The sound of the crunch of metal haunts my memories. If I don't choose to continue in recovery, then I might as well have died in that car accident. I could have died last September, too, but I'm still here. I'm still breathing.

That means one thing: Tara has to be right. There must be a reason for my existence.

I like the idea of taking it one day, one step, at a time. I know, from experience, that this can be an hour-by-hour, meal-by-meal, minute-by-minute kind of journey. And my first choice, right now—as I look at the faces of three strong women who surround me—is to choose life.

I choose to fight for my life, my health, and my future.

Maybe I do have a purpose. A purpose that can only be attained if I take that first step and release my hold of Anna's hand. So I do what I know to do in this moment.

I start to let go.

EPILOGUE

P*resent*

I RAISE the hammer above my head with my uncased left hand and hesitate. The motion is shaky and uncoordinated. I'm not sure if I can do this—not because I'm still getting used to doing everything left-handed. Kids ride bikes down the street while I sit in my empty driveway on the sun-warmed concrete. Self-conscious, I lower the hammer but still keep a grip on the smooth handle. Resting on the ground before me is my favorite teal and silver kaleidoscope that's embellished in sequins.

The words Kelly said to me on the day she gave me the journal runs through my thoughts.

"You see the world through kaleidoscope glasses, Ariel. It's easy for you to remember when your mom let you eat ice cream and Popsicles for breakfast, lunch, and dinner. But when you only think of that, you're blocking out memories of the fever that kept you bedridden. Which is why she was doing all she could to get you to

eat. Anna is the same way. Take the glasses off. See her for the part she truly played in your life."

Earlier, as I packed the items beneath my sink into a moving box, I came across my scale—the one I've forced myself to avoid since returning from treatment. Numbers flew through my brain and panic caused my heart to race at the thought of how much weight I might have gained. I closed my bathroom door, stripped down to my underwear, and stepped on top of the scale. I know I shouldn't have, but I couldn't help myself.

The number caused me to collapse onto the cold tile in tears. Anna's voice attempted to break through my wall—the one I've been trying to build with healthy thoughts about myself. I knew if I didn't do something soon, my progress would decline and I would spiral out of control once again. And I could not allow that to happen.

Anger, fear, and courage spurred me into action.

First, I threw the scale into the garbage bin. Second, I found the object that served as a constant reminder of Anna's lies and brought it outside along with the hammer.

And now the kaleidoscope sits in front of me, waiting to be smashed. I might not be able to tangibly rip Anna from my brain, but at least I can physically destroy every representation of her influence in my life.

You see, Anna, to me, is like a kaleidoscope. She's beautiful from the outside, and she promises to show me new ways of seeing the world. But then, when I actually view life through her eyes, all I can see are distorted colors and shapes of other people, food, and myself.

Anna has never been able to deliver on her promises. Of course, I know that destroying the kaleidoscope probably won't erase her from my life entirely—but I think it can at least offer me a sense of closure.

I squeeze my eyes shut and try to gather the resolve to break the kaleidoscope.

The sound of a car idling in front of my house prompts me to open my eyes. Jax turns off the engine of his Honda and steps out. He halts at the sight of me sitting in the driveway, a bludgeoning object in one hand and a child's toy on the ground in front of me.

"Should I be worried?" he asks with a laugh.

I hold the hammer in one hand and my injured arm against my stomach. I'm still getting use to wearing this sling. "What are you doing here?"

He takes an apprehensive step toward me. "Do I have permission to approach?"

I grin and roll my eyes. "Yes." I motion in front of me. "Sit." After Jax plops down across from me, I ask again, "What are you doing here?"

"The only communication I've had with you since the accident has come through texting." He shrugs. "I guess I just wanted to see how you were holding up."

I tap the head of the hammer against the concrete. "I've been busy. Mom and I are moving to a house that's twenty minutes away in a smaller neighborhood. She and Dad are selling this house. He'll live in Boston. The divorce is almost finalized."

Golden sunlight trickles through Jax's light brown hair, almost making it appear blond. "That sucks. I know the feeling." He nods toward the kaleidoscope, a smile lifting the corner of his lips. "So—am I allowed to ask what's happening here?"

The sequins that embellish the tube resemble a mermaid's tail. The kaleidoscope sits between us. It almost looks like we're about to play a game of spin the bottle. "Remember when we used to take apart our parent's old VCRs and portable CD players in the backyard? When we'd use tools from the shed behind your house?"

"Yeah . . . ?"

"We had a lot of fun," I muse. "I miss those days. Sometimes I wish we could be kids again."

He nods. "Me too."

"Things were simpler back then."

"That's an understatement." He laughs. "I can't believe we were in such a hurry to grow up. I'd give a week's pay just to have a day where I don't have to worry about school, work, groceries, or laundry." Jax seems caught up in the memories of childhood's simplicity for a moment—but then he seems to come back to reality as he glances back down at the hammer and tube between us. His brows draw together as he asks, "What does that have to do with anything though?"

I grin. "I want to dissect this kaleidoscope."

"Sorry. Still lost here. How is that going to—"

Before Jax can finish his question—and most importantly, before I can change my mind—I slam the hammer onto the tube, splitting it open.

Hard plastic pieces and beads spill across the ground like an exploding jar of sprinkles. But the ironic thing is, as soon as the kaleidoscope shatters, it's as if a piece of my broken mind snaps back into place.

I know Anna isn't entirely gone—but when the sound of plastic breaking registers in my ears, the distorted reflection of myself becomes fragmented. It's as if I've smashed the hammer against the mirror in my mind instead of the kaleidoscope.

"It's all a lie." A thrill, a sense of freedom, bolts through me as I say this—more to myself rather than to Jax. "It's always been a lie."

Poor Jax. Based on his confused expression, I wonder if he's starting to become even more seriously concerned for my mental health. "What are you talking about, Ariel?"

The sunlight causes the sequins to sparkle before me. I sift my fingers through the wreckage as glitter sticks to my fingers.

Observing the mess I've made, I admit with confidence, "I'm broken."

"No, you're not."

"Yes, I am."

"How?"

I look up at Jax. "Don't you get it? I've been living in this twisted reality." I bring the hammer to my temple. "There's been something in my brain that tells me to hate myself. Something that distorts the truth in my mind. But I don't want to keep living like that." I gesture toward the pieces before me. "My life is like that kaleidoscope."

"But that kaleidoscope is broken."

"Yeah," I say, standing. "That's kind of what I just said. I'm broken too."

Jax scrambles to his feet. "But if you're a broken kaleidoscope, then doesn't that mean you can see clearly now? You don't have to worry about distortion anymore."

Anna is the one who has become cracked and damaged. Shattering her has enabled parts of myself to come back together and into clearer focus. "I think I'm starting to see clearer."

Jax reaches out, and when I don't shrink away, he pulls me into a hug. Does he think I'm crazy? No, if he did, he'd be making excuses to jump in his Honda and speed off. "So what do you see now?" The tone he uses is gentle and reassuring.

My head rests on his shoulder, my cheek pressed against the warmth of his neck. I lift my head and catch a glimpse of my reflection in the windows of his car. But this time, I don't see an image of who I want to be; instead, I can only see my natural reflection which is untainted by Anna's distorted influence.

This within itself is a small victory. No, it's not necessarily a giant step from A to Z, but it's a small step from A to B. And it's these small steps that can lead me to freedom. I am now miles away from where I was last September, back when I fought for life the week before I entered WHT. The week of the hurricane.

My gaze remains trained on the glass as I study the lines and contours of my face. My cheeks are flushed with health, my eyes are bright, and my hair is thicker.

"I see myself now for who I really am."

My red lips part into a beautiful smile as happiness wells in my chest, satisfied with this reflection.

Despite this progress, I still might have to remind myself tomorrow that the girl who looks back at me is strong, healthy, and worth fighting for—but at least, in this moment, I can relax. I can find reassurance in the truth that there actually is a way forward. I haven't reached a dead end. And I don't need to see the whole path before I take that one step.

Because the only thing this journey requires of me is that I persevere. Hike one foot in front of the other, striving to allow each step to propel me forward—even if I might sometimes fall backward. I'm not strolling though. I'm hiking. This will require work, of course—but I'd much prefer the mountaintop views over the dark clouds caused from the hurricane of confusion.

I'm going up. I'm slipping. I'm picking myself back up and following the path less taken. The one that's filled with slippery slopes and occasional bruises—but also moments of rest that will allow me to take in the breathtaking sights.

I'm strong. I'm Ariel, and I will fight. I will find my purpose.

AUTHORS NOTE

Dear friend with an eating disorder,

I've been where you are. I'm familiar with the pain, frustration, and fear in which you struggle. I was diagnosed with anorexia at the age of fourteen and was unhappy with my body at the young age of seven. My self-destruction began when I accepted the false belief that I needed to change myself in order to be considered beautiful. So I started to make little choices regarding food—and that quickly spiraled out of control.

The idea of naming an eating disorder was first introduced to me when I was hospitalized for anorexia. Someone referred to an eating disorder as *Ed*, short for eating disorder. The name *Ed* sounded more like a creepy uncle twice removed rather than something I wanted to label my mental state. I never referred to my eating disorder as anything other than anorexia, but I could relate to feeling as though the disorder was a negative voice inside of my head, a voice that needed to leave.

Shortly after I took those first steps in recovery, I felt like I had a demon on one shoulder (the disorder) and an angel on the other (the truth). I felt like there were two voices warring over me, and it was my decision to either listen to the angel or the demon. Have you ever felt that way too? This war was also inspiration for Anna's character.

Like Ariel, I struggled with the desire to remove Anna from my life. My disorder was a part of me that I wanted to both kill and love at the same time.

I finally reached a point of fearing my disorder. Fortunately, I was accepted into a program known as Mercy Multiplied. (Mercy is a faith-based ministry that helps girls who have any type of life-controlling issue, and my eating disorder definitely had a controlling grip on my life.) I wanted to change, but I needed help. I needed *God's* help.

In one of Mercy's residential homes, I noticed something that has had an impact on me to this day. At the top of the second floor landing, a poster was nailed onto the wall. It showed a photo of a woman who held her pregnant stomach, and the verses from Psalm 139—which Tara quotes in the story —were displayed beneath.

"Oh yes, you shaped me first inside, then out;
    you formed me in my mother's womb.
    I thank you, High God—you're breathtaking!
    Body and soul I am marvelously made!
    I worship in adoration—what a creation!
    You know me inside and out,
    you know every bone in my body;
    You know exactly how I was made, bit by bit,
    how I was sculpted from nothing into something.
    Like an open book, you watched me grow from conception
to birth;
    all the stages of my life were spread out before you,
    The days of my life all prepared
    before I'd even lived one day."
    Psalm 139:13-16 (MSG)

Although the words were meant to inspire girls who had unplanned pregnancies, they still spoke to me in profound ways.

I'd grown up in a safe and loving church environment—but during the darkest days of my disorder, I struggled believing the concept that God could love me. If He did, why didn't He make me beautiful? I didn't understand why some girls could have perfect thin bodies, but I couldn't.

But as I walked up those stairs every day during my stay at Mercy and faced that poster, at some point, I started to believe those words. I started to believe that I was, in fact, created by God. I started to accept the truth that He doesn't make ugly things—or people.

After I graduated from the Mercy program, I continued to fight for recovery. The knowledge that God loved me meant so much to me, and that is why I wanted it to serve as a pivotal part of Ariel's journey too. Psalm 139 served as a monumental Scripture passage for me. I had to believe that I really was worth value before I could continue to walk in health.

I've been in recovery for over eleven years now, and each year has become easier. However, I'd be lying if I said that I didn't still struggle. Yes, I believe that God created me—but sometimes it's hard to *live loved*.

Lately, that has been my mantra. *Live Loved.* I have mentally wrestled with the idea and have attempted to find out what that means to me. I'm a Christian, but my life isn't perfect and I don't pretend it is. Sometimes, during my daily battles, my eating disorder is the one that wins—but the healthy part of me, the one that believes I am loved, wins more often. I'm on this journey together with you, and I do believe that we can make it to the other side.

If I could sit with you at Starbucks—sipping on my favorite chai latte or the Pink Drink—I would tell you this:

"Recovery is hard, yes—but it's worth it. There are girls who have gone before you who have fought and won or are still in war. Find a counselor and a close group of people who support you, a group that you can be 100 percent honest with. Don't beat yourself up when you make a mistake or lose a battle with Anna. If you've found that you have actually resurrected Anna, kill her—again, and again, and again. You can't live with one foot in recovery and one foot out. You have to go all in. And above all, know that you are beautiful and loved. Each body is different and unique. You are the only *you* in the world, and I think you are pretty awesome."

If you're willing to believe that you were, in fact, created, then I challenge you to find out more about what that means. Ask a friend who knows and believes that truth, or you can seek someone out in your community or church, someone who can help you to truly understand Psalm 139.

I have to remind myself of these truths too—again, and again, and again.

That's because life is a journey. So do what you love. Live, breathe, run, fly, swim, and embrace life to the fullest. You can make an impact, and you *can* touch a life in a way that nobody else can. You are someone who will make a difference. And yes, you are beautiful—simply because you are *you*.

Much love,

Shelbie Mae

P.S. I would love to connect! You can find me on Instagram, Facebook or Pinterest. You can also sign up for my newsletter at shelbie-mae.com. Thank you for reading *The Kaleidoscope Girl*!

ACKNOWLEDGMENTS

I told myself that if one of my books was ever published I'd thank God first. This work would not exist today if not for Him reaching into my brokenness and pulling me out of the dark and into light. This book is not mine, it's His.

I feel like an award winner trying to think of the best way acknowledge who I need to thank...

"I'd like to thank my mom, my dog, my best friend from elementary school..."

Okay, but in all seriousness, I DO need to thank my family. Seriously, I love everyone I'm related to. My parents, my sisters, my grandparents, aunts, uncles, cousins, and ALL my in-laws. I love you all. Family is one of the most important things in my life, so thank you for holding me up, making me laugh, and for all the hugs. I'm a hugger.

Thank you, Mason, for supporting me while I write on weekends instead of doing fun things with you. You've never doubted me. Instead you've asked what you can do to help and supported me in any way you can.

Thank you to my friends from Michigan and Florida (and other parts of the US) who have gotten excited with me as I continued this journey and want to read my book. You are awesome and your friendship means so much to me!

Thank you to Mrs. Gross, Mrs. Lowe, Mrs. Easling Mr. C, and the staff at Leland Public High School who humored me, read my first works, and didn't tell me I was a terrible writer. You certainly could have, but you fanned the flames of my dream and I never stopped working on writing since I was sixteen. You guided me in the right direction and didn't tell me my dream was unachievable.

Thank you to my college professor who also said my writing was good when it was still very much a work in progress.

Thank you to all the writers I reached out to over the years who wrote me back and told me to go for my dream. I still have my letter from Francine Rivers tucked into my beloved copy of *Redeeming Love.*

Thank you to the awesome Christian women who coached me and taught me about the craft of writing.

Thank you Tessa Hall for agreeing to help me edit my book.

Thank you Jamie for making an AMAZING cover.

And thank YOU for reading *The Kaleidoscope Girl*. You truly don't know how much it means to me. I'm humbled.

ABOUT

Shelbie Mae is married and lives with her husband and Boston Terrier between the states of Michigan, Florida and California. Besides writing she loves running, reading, hanging out with friends, being a small group leader, and baking fresh chocolate chip cookies. She loves making new friends and would love if you connected with her on social media.

Facebook: https://www.facebook.com/ShelbieMaeLiveLoved

Instagram: https://www.instagram.com/shelbiemaeliveloved/

Website: http://shelbie-mae.com/